Cibolero

**Center Point
Large Print**

**This Large Print Book carries the
Seal of Approval of N.A.V.H.**

Cibolero

Kermit Lopez

CENTER POINT PUBLISHING
THORNDIKE, MAINE

This Center Point Large Print edition is published in the year 2008 by arrangement with the author.

Copyright © 2007 by Kermit D. Lopez.

The text of this Large Print edition is unabridged. In other aspects, this book may vary from the original edition. Printed in the United States of America. Set in 16-point Times New Roman type.

ISBN: 978-1-60285-186-3

Library of Congress Cataloging-in-Publication Data

Lopez, Kermit.
   Cibolero / Kermit Lopez.--Center Point large print ed.
      p. cm.
   ISBN 978-1-60285-186-3 (lib. bdg. : alk. paper)
      1. Hunters--Fiction. 2. Kidnapping--Fiction. 3. New Mexico--History--1848--Fiction.
   4. Domestic fiction. 5. Large type books. I. Title.

PS3612.O625C53 2008
813'.6--dc22

2008000521

For my parents, Frances and Edward Lopez,
and Uncle Larry Lopez

No cruzamos la frontera; la frontera nos cruzó a nosotros.

—la gente de Nuevo México

CHAPTER I

Antonio Jose Baca gripped the hard, wooden handles of the plow firmly in his hands and shouted, "Ándale!" at the stubborn mule. The animal did not move.

Antonio heaved a sigh of frustration and hissed, "Terco!" He bent down, grasped a clod of dirt, and flung it at the animal. The mule lumbered forward, straining against the singletree plow. The blade of the plow cut through the fertile river bottom, forming a furrow as it turned over the sweet-smelling loam teeming with earthworms. Behind him a dozen noisy chickens scratched at the plowed field, in search of the burrowing worms.

Antonio's dark muscular arms and callused hands radiated strength. The reins, around his neck and under his arms, had long ago ceased chafing his skin. His torso, bronze from the neck down, suggested a life spent primarily in the open air and beneath the sweltering sun. Beads of sweat dripped from his forehead and soaked into the earth.

He reached the end of the field, where a small orchard grew, and released the plow, yanking the reins to signal the mule it was time to rest.

Pausing under the meager shade of an apple tree, he reached into the small sack hanging from his waist and grabbed a handful of seed corn. Then he began walking down the furrow, dropping three or four kernels with every step and pressing them into the ground with the toe of his boot. When he returned to the mule, the animal was fast asleep. Its head hung low and its rear foot dangled slack; its enormous penis almost touched the ground. Only its tail moved, frequently swatting at flies. Antonio woke the animal, maneuvered it around, and walked the plow to the opposite end of the field.

He started a new furrow, the plow turning the soil over, burying the seed. There was enough moisture in the warm earth to ensure the corn would sprout and push its way into the sun. Someday these clever americanos would invent a plow that could turn the soil over in the proper direction without having to waste time dragging it back to the beginning of a row. The Americans puzzled him; how could such a cruel, heartless people produce such wonderful implements and plentiful luxuries so cheaply that even he could afford them?

He repeatedly dragged the plow to the upper end of the field, plowing four more furrows on each pass, each time covering three furrows with turned-over soil and then planting corn in the fourth. Every so often, the mule lifted its tail and excreted several round "apples," further enriching the soil.

About once an hour, Antonio trudged to the nearby cottonwood-shaded creek, dipped a bucket in, took a big swig, and then watered the mule. By late afternoon his work was done. He unhitched the mule, wiped the plow blade clean with a burlap bag, and stripped off the moist, darkly stained harness, hanging it in a young apple tree. Then he led the animal to the stream and splashed water on its lathered flanks, currying it with a corncob. Although the animal obviously enjoyed the scrubbing, it was restless and visibly hungry, no doubt anticipating a supper of shelled corn and dry hay.

This was Antonio's favorite season. The air was hot in the sun, yet cool in the shade. Green cottonwood leaves dangled and vibrated in the late afternoon breeze, reflecting spikes of sunlight. A grove of snowy white *capulin* nestled among the cottonwoods, its wild cherry blossoms nurtured by the waters of the stream. The blossoms threw off a scent almost too sweet to endure.

In a week or two, this same stream would be filled with plentiful snowmelt draining from the towering Sangre de Cristo Mountains to the northwest. For the time being, however, the late spring sun bore down upon a dry valley. The sheltering canyon's walls, their ridges dotted with green piñon trees, reflected rays of copper and golden brown from the burning orb. The birds sang, the crows scolded, and the cicadas accompanied them with a steady hum. He could not imagine a better life!

Antonio looked back at the plowed field. The plow, dangling harness, and horse collar glinted in the sun. With a twinge of unease, he admitted that had the Americans not brought all these new things down from Missouri, life would be much more toilsome.

A growl in his belly abruptly turned his thoughts to

the supper waiting in the warm, safe kitchen of his three-room adobe house. His mouth watered at the thought of María's and Elena's cooking: a large stack of hot flour tortillas draped with a dish towel to keep them warm; a large pot of steaming beans; and cubes of venison swimming in bowls of red chile. He strode to the corral; locked in the mule; gave it a bucket of corn; and flung in several pitchforks of hay for the livestock. The pitchfork was another American-made implement, as was the barbed wire fencing the corral.

Antonio walked to the adobe house. A row of wooden vigas jutted horizontally from the walls to support the dirt roof. The adobe walls merged into a small *torreón,* a watchtower formation from which the *ranchito* could be defended in case of attack. In the five years since he had constructed the torreón, however, the immediate area had been spared any Indian raids, so the family now used the torréon for storing supplies and grain.

When Antonio stepped into the kitchen, María stopped him, holding her nose between her thumb and forefinger. She handed him a bucket of water, a towel, and a bar of store-bought soap, then gestured toward a clean shirt hanging on the nail sticking from the door jamb. Antonio laughed, grabbed the shirt, and went outside. He lathered himself from the bucket; rinsed and dried himself; put the shirt on; and re-entered the house, ready to devour María's cooking. He greeted her with an affectionate hug and a pat on her rear end. She blushed and slapped his hand.

Antonio smiled at his wife. María was a short woman in her mid-thirties with dark auburn hair and soft eyes, a contrast to the darker and harder features of her husband. And while María's eyes were light green, Antonio's were dark brown, almost matching the color of his hair.

Elena, their oldest child, placed a rolled tortilla on the cast-iron stove—what a change from the *comal* Antonio's mother had used all her life, from the one María had used for the first dozen years of their marriage! Antonio remembered the day he had proudly pried open the crate in which the Pennsylvania-made stove had traveled over a thousand miles from St. Louis. The stove's black firebox and oven contrasted sharply with the gleaming steel trim of its handles and legs, which María still polished daily. Antonio had saved the planks and nails for who-knew-what projects.

"Hola, Patrón," Joseph Lewis greeted him as Antonio sat down. Joseph was tearing a tortilla into pieces which could be used as spoons for scooping beans and chili from his tin plate.

"Hola, Pepé." Antonio nodded and continued in Spanish: "How's it going down at el rinconcito?" *Rinconcito* was Antonio's name for the nook in the small canyon a quarter mile to the south, where the land was covered with a delta of rich, crumply loam.

"Good, good. Got the beans and most of the squash hoed. Tomorrow I'll finish up and irrigate," Joseph answered and lapsed into silence. *A man of few words.*

Antonio liked that. Although he was at ease with the nineteen-year-old, lanky, yellow-haired, blue-eyed *gavacho,* who came from somewhere around Wisconsin, it always seemed unnatural to Antonio to hear an americano speak perfect New Mexican Spanish. Even more unnatural was the respect, even deference, which the younger man paid him.

Joseph had arrived in the territory at the age of fourteen and had drifted from job to job ever since, working first as a clerk for a Jewish shopkeeper in Las Vegas, and then for a Lebanese merchant in Santa Fe. Joseph had labored in a Mexican-owned saddle shop in Socorro, become a mule skinner and a master for wagon trains, and had worked at various other occupations including masonry and carpentry. In between he had lived with local people, learning the ways of the New Mexicans. He had taught himself to read first English, then Spanish. He could even add and subtract, rare among americanos as well as the New Mexicans.

One day, riding bareback on his skittish sorrel, Joseph had come to Antonio's ranchito to ask for a few months of work. Antonio had had no money to pay him, but had offered a share of whatever the small farm produced. Joseph had accepted on the spot, and months had turned into years. Now he had become part of the family. He often went with Antonio on trips to nearby villages or to the more distant Las Vegas. They both enjoyed the camaraderie. Antonio teased Joseph about his jittery sorrel with a Spanish saying:

"Alazán tostado, primero muerto que cansado!" Joseph liked that so much he translated it to every American he met: "Toasty-brown sorrel rather dead than exhausted."

During his first year at the ranchito, Joseph had slept in the adobe toolshed on a pile of sheep pelts, covered with a quilt Elena had pieced together from old scraps of cloth and stuffed with wool. During his second year, in his spare time and with Antonio's blessing, Joseph began building a small adobe house. Huffing and sweating, he hauled hundreds of pounds of flat ridge rock from the *ladera* to form the foundation. With bare feet he stumped the wet adobe earth, mixing in straw. He poured the mixture into wooden forms, producing adobe bricks that he baked in the sun. The two-room house began to take shape, adobe by adobe. Now, only the roof remained, which he would soon complete with logs and *latillas,* crisscrossing several layers of the slender sticks and covering them with eighteen inches of earth. He planned to fashion doors and window openings with inexpensive leftover lumber from St. Vrain's sawmill in Mora. Until he could afford glass, he would cover the windows with hide.

As Antonio ate, he glanced around the table with paternal satisfaction. Across from him sat his pride and joy, his eldest daughter Elena, a petite but strong girl—a woman, really—of seventeen years. She resembled him in most ways—black hair, brown eyes, and a hint of Indian ancestry—but her radiant beauty

13

came from María. Joseph called Elena "School-marm."

At the request of the territorial government, Elena had gone to school in Santa Fe for two years, her expenses paid. There she had lived in a boarding school and learned to read and write the American language, as well as to understand the rudiments of arithmetic and geography. She was then ready to teach others. While she had studied in Santa Fe, the government had built a small classroom here, a building of stone and adobe, with a corrugated metal roof and glass windows. It stood atop a ridge less than a half mile from Antonio's main house.

Under the agreement with the government, Elena was to teach the children in the valley, from La Cuesta to San Miguel del Vado, what she had learned. She earned a small salary, a godsend to her constantly cash-strapped family, by holding classes three times a week. School started late in the morning because many of the students, ranging in age from five to twelve, had to get up at five in the morning to travel the many miles to school. But all were eager to learn and carried their own lunches and water. Some came on horseback, others on *burros,* while most simply walked.

At the family dinner table, María sat to Antonio's right. Their other children, Mateo, Benito, Anita, and Gabriela, occupied the remaining chairs. Thirteen-year-old Mateo worked alongside his father in the fields and around the ranchito. Benito, at age nine,

14

went to Elena's school each class day after he finished his morning chores. Anita, almost six, would start next year, while Gabriela, at three, still had several years to enjoy unfettered freedom, chasing butterflies and dipping her toes and fingers in the stream. Once there had been a sixth child, a boy who had died as an infant, about two years before Mateo was born.

As the family ate their meal, Antonio said, "I need to buy some more seed. There's still more plowing and planting to do."

"Las Vegas?" María asked.

"I'm riding out there tomorrow morning. With any luck, I'll be back the following day."

Mateo interrupted, "Can I go with you, Papa?"

Antonio smiled and slowly shook his head, "No, no. I want you here. You have chores tomorrow, working on those fence posts. You can help Pepé too."

Antonio sensed some anxiety in María, who was always a bit uneasy when Antonio left home. He added, "I'll only be gone one night."

"But what about the Comanche troubles to the east?"

Antonio smiled reassuringly. "Those are only rumors. The only Indian around these parts is your old Tío Armando up in San Jose."

María smiled at the mention of Tío Armando, who was named after her Pueblo Indian grandfather from Santo Domingo.

"And besides," said Antonio, "the Comanches don't come this way anymore. They only roam out on the llano fighting the American army."

"El llano," Mateo said with a glint in his eye. "The land of the Ciboleros."

Antonio nodded with a smile, anticipating what the children were about to ask him.

"Tell us again about the Ciboleros," Elena added. "I like your stories, Papa."

"Me, too," Joseph added with an appreciative glance.

Although Antonio enjoyed telling his children the tall tales from his youth, right now he was tired and simply wanted to finish his meal and rest. "No, not now. Maybe later. Let's just finish eating."

Elena pointed at a long wooden lance that hung on the wall, an heirloom from another time and place. The lance was taller than a man, and the metal from which it was formed was strong and rugged. The tip of the lance was configured into a sharp protruding spear of metal.

"You were a Cibolero," Elena stated proudly. "A hunter of the llano."

"Yes," Antonio said. "I *was*. But that was a long time ago, and I was much younger." He added wistfully: "And much more foolish than I am now."

"Y más guapo," María said with a smile. The children giggled and Joseph grinned.

The family finished eating. Anita and Elena began picking up the dishes. Benito, who thought himself a man, made no move to help with the "women's work." His father glared at him; Benito hurriedly arose and began clearing the table.

While Anita and Benito washed the dishes, Elena lit

the coal-oil lamp—an American invention that lengthened the days—and moved to a small desk to prepare the lessons for her next class, which would meet in two days. Joseph sidled up to her. She responded with muted giggles and whispering.

As he conversed with María, Antonio kept a protective eye on his daughter. What was going on between Elena and Joseph? Last autumn he had sent them to pick fruit and found them chasing each other through the orchard, laughing and tumbling. Irritated, he had ordered them back to work; the fruit had to be picked, cooked, and dried before the winter snows came. Chastised, the young couple had picked up the buckets and returned to their task, but they had continued throwing glances of delight at each other. Antonio had thought of telling Joseph to leave, but the young man had become almost irreplaceable around the farm. Besides, it was all childish play, or so Antonio told himself.

At daybreak the next morning, Antonio prepared to depart for Las Vegas. While the children slumbered in the small room adjacent to the kitchen, María prepared him a hearty breakfast of *chaquegüe,* a cornmeal mush, to keep his hunger at bay until at least midday. By that time, he expected to be well on his way. His route would take him past the small community of Los Montoyas and briefly onto the flat plains that spread eastward from the Sangre de Cristo Mountains.

After Antonio finished breakfast, he stepped into the crisp morning air and watched the sun rise slowly. A hint of dew covered the landscape, and the scent of freshly cut piñon drifted from a nearby pile of wooden logs. The sunrise cast a pink haze across the ranchito and the surrounding canyon walls. A rooster crowed in the cool morning air as Antonio loaded several empty crates onto the flat wooden planks of the wagon that would carry the seed and other supplies back from Las Vegas.

Antonio often made this journey. Though he preferred to avoid too many trips away from home, especially during the planting season, he was confident that María and Joseph could run the ranchito during the day or two he was gone. As soon as he returned, they would begin irrigating. Antonio hoped the autumn harvest would provide enough food to see them through the next year. They had almost starved several years earlier when the harvest was poor; Antonio had been forced to slaughter almost all his animals to feed the family.

As Antonio finished hitching up his mule, María put a cloth sack on the wagon bed and said, "I fixed you some frijolitos. There's *carne seca* and tortillas too."

Antonio leaned forward and gently kissed her forehead. He put his arms around her and hugged her close.

She held him tightly. "Be safe," she whispered.

Antonio slipped from her arms and pointed at the gun in the holster at his waist. "I'll be fine."

"I worry about you riding alone. I'd feel much better if Pepé could go with you."

"Pepé has work to do. Stop worrying, María."

"I'll try."

Antonio placed several fraying leather sacks in the back of the wagon and mounted the cart. He grabbed the mule's reins and maneuvered the wagon onto the narrow dirt path that led toward the crest of the surrounding canyon. The cart's wheels screeched in the dirt.

María turned and walked back toward the house. A full day of work and chores awaited her and the family.

At midday, Mateo finished firming up several wooden fence posts and went to feed the goats. He planned to help Joseph over at el rinconcito when these tasks were complete.

As he went about his chores, Mateo thought about the plans his father had made for the corral and the ranchito. Antonio wanted to graze sheep in the upper elevations of the canyon, beneath a series of meadows fed by a Río Pecos tributary. The new corral would eventually be used to pen in at least part of the flocks during shearing. "Perhaps by the end of summer we can purchase the sheep," Antonio had told his son recently. Raising sheep would help offset bad crop years. Mateo hoped to have most of the smaller fence posts ready by the time Antonio returned from Las Vegas.

Elena stirred a large pot of laundry soap, made from animal lard and lye, near the entrance to the house. The three smaller children and their mother were inside.

As Mateo fed the goats, a reflection caught his peripheral vision, a brief glint from somewhere up near the rim of the canyon. Mateo stopped and scanned the rim. He did not see anything unusual. Perhaps it was merely the reflection of some shiny rock. His attention returned to the fence posts.

Mateo heard something and again stopped and carefully searched the canyon walls with his eyes. A faint echo of voices and, the scraping of horse hooves against dirt and rock drew his attention. The sounds gradually became louder and more distinct.

Mateo raised his head slightly and stared at the northern ridge of the canyon, squinting against the reflection of the noon sun off the cliffs. A group of men on horseback appeared on the canyon rim. He counted six individuals but could not discern their still-distant faces.

The horsemen advanced down the narrow trail that hugged the northern ridge, the same trail that had led Antonio out of the canyon that morning. As they drew closer, Mateo could see they looked tired and disheveled. Their clothes were caked with dust and dirt. *Vaqueros?* he thought. Several large ranchos had recently been established on the pastures to the east.

María came out of the house as Elena paused in her stirring to watch the horsemen slowly descending the trail down the side of the bluff. Mateo wished his father were here now. *Papa would know about such men.*

Travelers did often pass by the ranchito on their way into the valley, and often stopped to ask for a cup of water or something to eat. Antonio and María would always prepare a small meal for the strangers.

Now, as the party of horsemen drew nearer to the ranchito, Mateo instinctively moved away from the fence posts and walked toward where Elena stood by the house. The horses stepped slowly onto the grounds of the ranchito, kicking up a small trail of dust. The six horsemen came to a stop a few feet from Mateo and his sister. Mateo saw their faces clearly now and could tell these men were not vaqueros from any of the nearby ranchos.

CHAPTER II

The men were foreigners, which was obvious not so much from their complexions, but from their language and mannerisms. Two had scraggly yellow beards, and the other three had varying degrees of beard growth. *Gringos,* thought Mateo. To the people of the surrounding villages and communities, a "gringo" was any foreigner, most of whom were americanos. Many had come to the region in recent years, but Mateo had not had much direct interaction with them, except for Joseph, and Mateo did not really think of Joseph as a gringo. Joseph was simply "Pepé," a member of the family.

Antonio had told his son how their own ancestors had made the long arduous journey to this land from Nueva España—México—more than two centuries ago. Nuevo México had been a province of México in Antonio's youth and a part of distant España in his father's day. The Americans had conquered the region some twenty years earlier, but, like most New Mexicans, Mateo and his family lived in communities that had always been relatively isolated from the larger world and from men such as these strangers.

The horses filed into the ranchito in a column. The man on the lead horse, who seemed to be in charge, removed his hat and nodded at Mateo and Elena. Mateo recoiled slightly at a strong acrid scent; apparently these men had not bathed for a while.

The man said something in English, to which Mateo shrugged to indicate he did not understand. The man then spoke in broken Spanish: "Agua, por favor."

Mateo nodded. "Sí." Although Mateo's grasp of their language was limited, he understood that these horsemen wanted to rest here. He pointed in the direction of the partially completed fence posts and a nearby trough of water. An open well, surrounded by a ring of rocks was next to the trough, and an empty bucket with a rope tied to it sat on the ground next to the well.

The man nodded and then turned to speak to his companions. Mateo listened closely, but could not make out what they said.

When María heard the commotion outside, she

opened the front door and watched the six strangers ride into the ranchito. Elena who was already outside stirring the pot of boiling laundry soap, moved away from the pot to stand next to her mother.

As the men dismounted and tied their horses to the fence posts, María looked at her son and said anxiously, "Come here."

The boy darted toward his mother and sister.

The lead horseman and two of his companions now stood beside their horses, checking their gear and saddles. The other three men scooped water from the well. Each took his turn drinking vigorously from a tin cup they had found inside the empty bucket. Then they filled their canteens.

J. D. Calhoun, a tall, burly man with tired eyes and a face burned from too many days in the sun, took another gulp of water from the tin cup. "Nice little spread here."

Hugh McNally, a second gringo, nodded. "Sure is, J. D."

"You think Captain Russell can hear us?" asked the third man, Kyle Adams. Kyle was about twenty-two or twenty-three years old—though even he wasn't certain of his exact age—and stood shorter than either of the other two men, thin and gangly with a neck that seemed more a stick than actual flesh and blood.

Calhoun shook his head. He scratched his full beard and looked angrily at the lead horseman. "Look at him. Captain Russell's too busy talking to the preacher to mind us."

"You think the captain knows what he's doing?" Kyle asked.

"I reckon we'll know soon enough, once we get back out onto those plains," McNally said. "He managed to get us west across the panhandle in one piece. I would think he can lead us back east."

"Right through Comanche country," Kyle added.

"Russell has his head up his ass," Calhoun spat. "We ought to just move down the Río Grande to El Paso."

"But we'd run into Apaches in that direction," Kyle said.

Calhoun removed a thin metal flask from an inner pocket of his shirt. He opened it, took a swig, and said to Kyle and McNally, "Have another drink."

Kyle snickered. "We've been sipping this brew for miles. What is it they call it?"

Calhoun said with a slight grin, "Taos Lightning. I should have bought more of it in Santa Fe. We're getting low."

"Russell knows we've been sipping this stuff. I'm surprised he ain't said anything," McNally commented.

"It doesn't matter if Captain Russell knows," Calhoun snapped. "What I drink or don't drink of is none of his goddamned business."

McNally grabbed the flask. "Watch your language J. D. If there's one thing the preacher don't approve of, it's taking the Lord's name in vain."

24

"The preacher don't approve of a lot of things," Calhoun said. He glanced at the adobe house. "Particularly these kinds of people."

Kyle bit his lip. "The sooner we're back home, the better."

"Amen to that," McNally added, taking another sip from the flask. "I only hope Russell is up for it."

"Well, he brought us all the way to Santa Fe," Kyle said. "I reckon he'll manage to get us back to Texas. I trust the Captain."

Calhoun snorted. "If we ever get around to heading back. It's been three weeks since we left Waco, and we still ain't caught that colored boy yet. We chased him halfway across the panhandle, right through Comanche land. Had his trail until we got into this damned land."

"Well, this ain't Texas," McNally said.

Calhoun nodded. "That's how come we lost Bill's trail."

"I hate to admit it, but our boy Bill is long gone by now." There was a hint of admiration in McNally's voice. "That boy was one hell of a horse thief. Covered the ground from Waco up to Dallas." McNally glanced at the lead horseman and their other two companions, still standing near the horses. "It's time to go back. Ol' Bill has done disappeared someplace here in New Mexico territory."

Calhoun shook his head as he surveyed the ranchito. "You know, it's just *not* right."

McNally raised an eyebrow. "What ain't right? That our boy Bill got away?"

25

"No, I'm not thinking about that."

"Well, what's not right?"

Calhoun continued to study the fields, the adobe house, and the surrounding countryside. "Look at this place."

Kyle and McNally shrugged their shoulders and looked blank.

"Are you blind?" Calhoun growled. "Nice chunk of land here. Somehow it don't seem *right* for greasers to have such a nice little spread."

"Why don't you take it for yourself?" McNally teased.

"How am I supposed to do that?"

"My brother got his hands on some of the best land in South Texas, thousands of acres." McNally grinned. "Some greaser families were occupying *that* land, too. But the Rangers helped chase those people out of there. My brother ended up with the land and a nice hacienda. You ought to be able to do the same damned thing in New Mexico. A man could have a good life here."

"Not a bad idea," mused Calhoun. He glanced at Mateo and María, who still stood cautiously near the entrance to the adobe house. Curiosity and apprehension were written on their faces.

Calhoun stared back at María and remarked, "Good-looking woman."

He then caught a glimpse of Elena as she moved into his view from behind her mother. Calhoun's eyes widened, and he smiled a gap-toothed grin. "Well, well, what do we have here?"

"I wouldn't mind having some of that," McNally commented.

Calhoun took another gulp from the flask, as if to enhance his courage. "Who's to say we can't?" He closed the flask and placed it back in his shirt pocket. He strode toward the family. "It's our due, ain't it?"

María had kept a watchful and suspicious eye on the horsemen since they arrived. At first, the three men standing beside the tired horses had seemed caught up in a world of their own, deep in conversation, oblivious even to their three companions beside the well. But the flask they were sharing obviously contained something other than water—and they had obviously had quite a lot of it.

"Borrachos," María said angrily.

Then the largest of the three men glanced at Elena. María quickly said to her daughter, "Go take care of the children."

Elena opened the door and hurried into the house. María caught a glimpse of Gabriela's and Anita's frightened faces, and of Benito standing protectively next to his younger sisters, before slamming the door closed behind Elena.

María felt her hands tremble and her heart race as the tall, burly gringo strode toward her, his two companions following. "Mateo," she said, and then realized her son had disappeared.

María backed up to the boiling pot of *jabón*. Beside the cooking laundry soap sat a bucket filled with lye.

A large metal spoon leaned against the wall nearby.

The drunken gringo now stood in front of María. He muttered something she did not understand and seized one of her forearms. María struggled against his grip. "No!" she screamed.

She felt other hands paw at her and heard inebriated voices and scornful laughter. She prayed that Elena had locked the front door, that the children had taken refuge in the torreón adjoining the side room.

María stumbled and fell as the men surrounded her. She grabbed the metal spoon, plunged it into the bucket, and flung lye blindly at the three men. One screamed as it splattered on his face.

Suddenly, María heard a thundering noise and caught an acrid smoke scent. She turned to the left to see Mateo standing five feet away, near the corner of their home where a curved adobe wall merged into the torreón. He was holding a rifle.

Mateo yelled in Spanish, "Leave her alone!"

The three men sprang aside. María saw past them to the other three, fanning out from their positions near the horses. Their guns were drawn and they stared in bewilderment.

Then the room erupted in confusion and panic. Another gunshot shattered the air. María shrieked as she saw Mateo collapse in the dirt by the torreón. As she lunged toward him, she felt a pair of hands grasp her throat.

María jammed her elbow backward, connecting with her attacker's own throat. There was a hiss of air and a muttered curse. María twisted free and spun around to see the large stranger glaring at her, rage burning in his glazed eyes. His fist crashed against her face. María moaned and sank into blackness.

Calhoun rubbed his throbbing neck as he watched the woman crumble to the ground like a rag doll. Then he remembered the girl inside the adobe house. *My reward,* he thought. He stumbled forward to the front door. McNally and Kyle followed him.

Someone shouted, "J. D.! Get back here!" Disoriented, his mind focused on his objective, he ignored the voice.

His mind tried to focus on the girl inside the adobe house. *My reward,* he thought. He gripped his revolver and stood in front of the door. The sounds of someone fumbling with a lock came from within.

Calhoun lunged forward and threw the full force of his large body into the door. It flew open and collided with the person struggling to lock it. He saw the girl stumble backward toward a table surrounded by wooden chairs. Her head hit one of the chair legs and her body crashed to the floor. As Calhoun stepped forward, she lay motionless.

McNally and Kyle pushed past Calhoun. McNally rubbed the burns on his face from the lye María had flung at him. His bloodshot eyes watered. "Damned Mexican bitch!" he cursed.

"Is the girl dead?" Kyle gasped.

Calhoun shook his head and said with a smirk, "No,

she ain't dead." He rubbed his eyes and stared down at the unconscious girl. "She's coming with us. When she's awake, we're gonna have ourselves a good ol' time."

Chapter III

Antonio was only five miles from home. The ride to Las Vegas and back had passed quickly. He chewed the last of the delicious carne seca María had packed the previous morning. Its dry, flaky texture reminded him of the days when most of the carne seca in New Mexico came from el Cibolo, the buffalo that had once roamed the great Llano Estacado. The Pueblo Indians had called this mighty animal Shiwana in their Tiwa language. Antonio shook his head sadly and recalled the vast herds of buffalo that once roamed the eastern plains of New Mexico.

He pulled back slightly on the mule's leather reins and nudged the animal forward with a soft kick in its side. Not far ahead lay his ranchito in the little canyon that fed the Río Pecos and stretched on to the valley where the little village of La Cuesta lay. That town sat on a bluff overlooking the Río Pecos, a position that offered it natural protection not only from the elements, but also from the occasional Indian raid.

From this vantage point, Antonio could see eastward to the vast expanse of the Llano Estacado, the land his people had once called home. Almost since Coronado had explored this land three hundred years earlier in his quest for the mythical seven cities of Cibola, the Spaniards and their descendants had hunted in the Llano and considered it their territory. The hated Tejanos, however, had now appropriated much of the Llano, forcing the Comanches from their traditional settlements and hunting the buffalo into extinction.

To the northwest rose the Sangre de Cristo Mountains, and to the southwest towered the rugged spires of the Sandía and Manzano Mountains above the middle Río Grande Valley, where Antonio's ancestors had lived. Beyond the valley lay the remaining New Mexico territory, which included the lands of the Navajo and the Hopi and the frontier of the region known as California.

Antonio felt satisfied that he had acquired just the right amount of seed to finish the planting. He had made it to Las Vegas on the evening of the previous day, and had purchased seed and supplies from his old friend, Armando Tafoya. Armando ran a small store that served most of *la gente* in Las Vegas, leaving the larger, better-supplied stores to cater to the gringo interlopers who had moved into the area in recent years.

Antonio's carreta creaked as it ambled forward, pulled by the tired gray mule. The two flat wooden wheels turned on a cottonwood axle. The squeaking noise they made sparked further memories of a past that was no more. Antonio recalled his youth in the bosques of Atrisco, so many years ago. . . .

"Antonio, move!" his mother called.

The five-year-old boy froze as the carreta his father had released from the large-horned ox's harness rolled backward. Antonio's father snatched him away barely in time to prevent him from being crushed beneath the large wooden wheel.

Antonio saw the panic in his mother's eyes quickly yield to relief, then anger. She ran to him and began scolding him harshly. Tears came to his eyes.

His mother instantly seemed sorry. She threw her arms around her young son in a warm embrace. "No llores, mi hijito," she said. "Don't cry."

Antonio lived with his parents and his six brothers and sisters in Atrisco, a tiny hamlet on the western banks of the Río Grande. Atrisco, only a few leagues from the small collection of adobe huts known as *la villa de Alburquerque* on the eastern side of the river, resembled a series of isolated estancias or farms more than a village. Antonio's father Francisco worked a tract of land that hugged the Río Grande Bosque, *bosque* being the Spanish word for "forest." This was the same land Antonio's grandfather and great-grandfather had farmed.

This part of Atrisco had been known as Los Bacas since the 1600s, when the Baca family had received the land grant that hugged the Atrisco bosque. The Bacas had lived in New Mexico since the time of Oñate, the conquistador who brought the first Spanish colony to New Mexico.

Cristobal Baca, a direct ancestor of Antonio's father, had come with Juan de Oñate in 1599 to settle the lands of Nuevo México. The Bacas eventually spread throughout most of the villages and towns of New Mexico. Their land grant had extended several leagues northward from Atrisco along the western banks of the Río Grande Bosque. While tiny in comparison to many other New Mexican land grants, especially the great Sangre de Cristo land grant to the north and the Luna and Tomé land grants further south, the Baca grant made up for that in the generous capacity of its fertile ground. Antonio had happy memories of his early childhood in Atrisco, even though life in the province of New Mexico had been a constant struggle for survival. His family had survived for generations in this harsh land. *El Reyno de Nuevo México* had been the northernmost frontier province of the Spanish Empire and later of México, a buttress against nomadic Indian raiders from the north and west and against a small but steadily increasing flow of interlopers from the east.

Antonio's father and mother had worked hard to keep their children fed and clothed. When the crops were poor, his father and uncles worked for *los ricos* at Los Lunas or Los Corrales, and were paid in sacks of corn or wheat.

Antonio's father, Francisco, was a stern man with little patience for idleness. Francisco's life centered on his family, his land, and the Holy Mother Church. Francisco was a Penitente, a member of that secretive order of New Mexico Catholics who kept the faith alive in a land where few priests were found. Antonio could still recall some of the many *alabados* chanted by his father, who vanished for a few days each spring, during the holy season, to a Penitente morada south of Atrisco.

Antonio's mother, María Elena, in whose honor his firstborn daughter had been named, was a small woman with soft dark eyes and a warm smile. Her hands were strong from daily chores, from picking chiles and tomatoes from the fields and from plastering the adobe house with mud. Men and women in the frontier settlements of Nuevo México shared the field work. In later years, Antonio would smile sentimentally, wondering how such a small woman had given birth to so many children. Perhaps her strength was derived from her role as a *curandera*. He recalled her walks into the Sandía and Manzano Mountains to search for the precious roots and herbs that filled her hearth; the pungent aroma of boiled *oshá* or *plumajillo* often lingered in the air when a family member was ill.

In late spring, the waters of the Río Grande swelled with snowmelt, sometimes overflowing the riverbanks and flooding adjacent farms and villages, such as Atrisco. Each evening as the sun dipped below the western horizon, Antonio heard the waters of the mighty river roaring downstream, carrying chunks of cottonwood trees and the carcasses of animals drowned upstream near the northern villages of Chimayo and Santa Cruz de la Canada, or near the Indian pueblos of Santo Domingo and Cochiti.

Each summer, the children worked in the fields alongside their parents or tended flocks of sheep in the barren hills east of Alburquerque. Often left alone to guard the sheep, the children were ever vigilant of incursions from the nomadic Navajo Indians to the west.

On those rare days when the work was light, the children ran barefoot among the green cottonwood groves of the Río Grande bosque and drank from the cool waters of las acequias, the communal system of irrigation ditches that maintained the precarious water supplies of the Río Abajo, the middle Río Grande Valley between Socorro and la capital, Santa Fe. At harvest time in the early autumn, the delicious aroma of roasting green chiles wafted through the air of Atrisco and among many of the small farms of the Río Abajo.

Antonio also had memories of tragedy in the family. He vaguely remembered the deaths of his two older brothers, the twins Mañuelito and Pablito, from smallpox. He recalled his mother's torn face and his father's head bowed in sadness as they stood beside two little crosses in a green field near the bosque. The same pox, which Antonio somehow managed to avoid catching, had left his younger brother, Felipe, with a scarred face, but that never seemed to quell Felipe's youthful enthusiasm.

And among the tragedies, the hardships, and the pleasures, one person stood out as especially strong in Antonio's memory—the rock of granite that was his *abuelo,* his grandfather, Donaciano Baca. Donaciano had appeared frail at first glance but was actually a colossus of energy and vigor. The old man had lived with his son's family, and his grandchildren had idolized him.

It was from Donaciano that Antonio had first learned of the Ciboleros, they famed buffalo hunters and expert horsemen of the boundless Llano Estacado far to the east of the Sandía Mountains. Old Donaciano had at one time been Cibolero, although for many years, he had lived the settled life of a farmer it Atrisco. The life of the Cibolero had remained burned into Donaciano's memories, stirring his blood with the vigor of his youth and calling to him like a lost love. Antonio spent many winter nights sitting by a warm fire, listening to the stories of the Ciboleros and their encounters with herds of buffalo a million strong. The old man also told long and dramatic tales of the Comanches, the feared horse people of the llano.

But Antonio's father frowned upon the Ciboleros, considering them an unsettled lot as wild as the wind and as unpredictable as the late summer dust storms that yearly enveloped Atrisco. It was not the kind of life Antonio's father desired for his children.

"Stay with the land," Francisco told Antonio. "Don't follow in the footsteps of your abuelo and Tío Tomás." Antonio's Tío Tomás, a Cibolero, had been gone for many months each year, usually during the fall.

Antonio viewed his uncle as an almost legendary

figure, a navigator upon an endless ocean of earth and rock and grasslands that the nuevomexicanos knew as the Llano Estacado, or simply the *llano*. To Antonio, the llano was a mystical land that filled him with a sense of freedom.

Horses and mules often came in from the llano in those days pulling carretas packed high with tons of buffalo meat, much of which had been dried to make carne seca. The delicious dry buffalo meat, with its savory flavor, was sold throughout New Mexico and taken by el Camino Real—the royal road into the province of Chihuahua. It would eventually find its way a thousand miles south in the capital of New Spain, Mexico City. It had been that way for as long as anyone could remember, since before the time of the celebrated Governor De Vargas and the Reconquista of 1690, as old Francisco had explained to his grandchildren.

Now, Antonio guided his mule-drawn wagon onto the tapered dirt trail that hugged the ridge of the canyon. The ranchito soon came into full view. Soon he would be home with his family.

The late afternoon sun inched its way down the western horizon, painting the blue sky with shades of pink, orange, and red. The canyon gleamed golden brown in the light.

Below, streams trickled toward the Pecos River valley. The snowmelt from the Sangre de Cristos was good this year. Antonio thought of the old, shadowy people who had long ago occupied the Pecos Pueblo near where the snowmelt originated, whose descendants now lived west of the Sangre de Cristos. *Those are my people, too,* Antonio thought. *"Tenemos la misma sangre . . . sangre de indio,"* old Francisco Baca had said. "We have the same blood . . . the blood of the Indian."

As Antonio made his way down the rim of the canyon, he could see no more of the ranchito than a few small structures, yet something was not quite right. Mateo had not finished the fence posts, which was not like him. And Antonio could see only one horse in the corral. When Antonio had left, two horses, which were usually inseparable, were at home.

Then Antonio saw two horses tied to the hitching post near his well. One of those horses belonged to their nearest neighbor, Eugenio Tafoya, who lived on a rancho some ten miles to the west. Like Antonio, Eugenio was a subsistence farmer who made his livelihood from the land. Several years ago when crops were poor, Eugenio and Antonio had worked together as seasonal vaqueros on local ranchos owned by los ricos.

Antonio urged his mule forward, his stomach churning with uneasiness. Reaching the house, he quickly dismounted and tied the mule to the hitching post. Leaving the carreta where it was, he hurried to the front door. Voices came from within the house. He cautiously pushed the door open.

Inside, he saw his two small daughters sitting at the

table with Benito. They smiled when he entered, but there was an uncomfortable feeling in the room. Antonio glanced at the old woman standing near the table, serving *pan* and *quelites*. He recognized her as Señora Tafoya, Eugenio's mother. *Why is she here?*

Antonio made himself smile pleasantly. "Buenos días, señora."

The old woman did not respond; she hardly seemed to notice him. Her usually cheerful face was grim and sad. *What is wrong?*

Then two men appeared from the house's other room. Each had a hat in his hand as if preparing to depart.

"Eugenio," Antonio said softly.

The tall, thin man in his thirties reached out to shake Antonio's hand. "I'm very glad you've returned," he said. Eugenio then motioned toward the man beside him, an older man of perhaps seventy years. "Antonio, you remember Father Abeyta." The old priest from La Cuesta was one of the last native priests still practicing in New Mexico.

"Hello, my son," the priest said gently.

Since the coming of the americanos into this land, most of the native priests had been driven from the Church by Bishop Lamy, the despised Frenchman from the East. Now residing in Santa Fe, the bishop had come to New Mexico after the American occupation to impose a "less objectionable" form of Catholicism.

"Hola, Padre," Antonio said.

Eugenio cleared his throat and said slowly, "There were some troubles while you were away." He paused, as if not wanting to continue.

"Go on," Antonio said.

"Your son—" Eugenio stopped.

Antonio waited.

Eugenio took a deep breath. "Mateo was shot."

Antonio felt his heart drop and blood rush from his face. "I . . . I don't understand."

"Your boy was shot," Eugenio said again. "He's alive, but unconscious." Antonio looked about the room. "Where is he? Where is María?"

"They're in the other room." Eugenio put his hand on Antonio's shoulder. "There's more, Antonio."

"Tell me."

"María was attacked."

Antonio felt anger and fear well within him. *This is madness,* he thought. He took a quick step toward the next room. "I need to see them."

"In a moment," Eugenio said. "But there is something else."

Dear God, Antonio thought.

"They took Elena."

Antonio's head swam with bewilderment and shock. The whole world suddenly seemed unreal. He pushed blindly past the other two men into the small adjoining room.

Mateo lay on a small wooden cot in the corner. A cool rag covered his forehead, and a makeshift bandage draped one edge of his temple.

María sat on a wooden chair beside her son. A large purple bruise extended along one side of her face. She looked numbly at Antonio.

Antonio went to her side and knelt to embrace her. They were both shaking.

"The bullet didn't pierce his body," María whispered. "But it did graze his head." She pointed at the bandage. "Señora Tafoya bathed Mateo's wound with her yerbas."

Antonio's voice trembled. "Will he live?"

"We won't know until morning. He seems to be running a fever." María began to cry softly. "It happened so fast. I couldn't fight them off."

"It's not your fault," Antonio said. "I shouldn't have gone to Las Vegas. I should have been here."

"No, Antonio. You can't blame yourself for what happened."

He shook his head and lowered it, unable to bear the sorrow in his wife's eyes. Then he thought of his daughter. "Elena?"

"She was gone by the time I came to. She hid the children under the floorboards, but didn't have time to join them. The little ones told me the intruders took Elena. They saw everything from beneath the cracks in the floor."

"Los Comanches . . ." Antonio said angrily.

María shook her head slowly. "No. Not Comanches."

Antonio was surprised. "Are you certain?"

"Oh yes."

"If not Comanches, then who were these animals?"

"Tejanos," she said, and then repeated, "Tejanos . . ."

Eugenio Tafoya stepped into the room and apologized for the interruption. He stepped aside as another figure emerged from the shadows behind him. "Pepé," Antonio said softly.

The younger man's eyes sagged and his face was covered with blotches of dirt, dust, and sweat. "I don't know what to say, Antonio," he whispered. "I'm so sorry." Joseph's eyes filled with tears. "I was out at el rinconcito when I heard the gunshots. I ran to the house as fast as I could. But by the time I got here, Elena was gone."

"Joseph rode to my place to get help," Eugenio said. "He told us what happened."

Antonio placed one hand on Joseph's shoulder. "Thank you, Pepé."

Eugenio added, "Pepé has been out in the countryside for hours, looking for any sign of the horsemen."

"I lost their tracks above the canyon rim," Joseph said grimly.

"Antonio," Eugenio said, "Father Abeyta and I are leaving now. My mother will remain here for the night. She can stay for a few days if you need her."

"I'm grateful," Antonio said, the thought of his daughter's suffering shifting helplessly through his mind.

"We've sent word of Elena's kidnapping to San Miguel and Las Vegas," Eugenio said.

"So what will be done?"

"I honestly don't have an answer for you, Antonio. Those bandits were gringos. I doubt we'll get much help from the americano officials in Las Vegas or Santa Fe."

Antonio recognized the truth in his friend's words.

Eugenio continued, "The gringos don't like the thought of armed mexicanos roaming the land. And even if we can organize men with the authority to track down these strangers, it could take days."

"So what do you suggest I do?" Antonio snapped.

"Be patient, my friend. Look to your family here. I'll return with news in the morning."

As Eugenio and the priest departed, Antonio went to his son's bedside and, weeping helplessly, gently kissed Mateo's forehead.

CHAPTER IV

Captain Travis Russell of the Texas Rangers was lost. The Llano Estacado was too large and mysterious to fathom. To his fellow riders, the area was devoid of life or utility. They held it in disregard largely because much of the land was still dominated by Comanches. And Russell dared not allow the men under his command to know he had lost his bearings. Especially not that troublemaker Calhoun. Russell reasoned that if the group continued riding southeast, they would eventually return to friendlier territory.

Russell was of medium height and build, with sandy

brown hair and blue eyes. At thirty, he was already a veteran of numerous campaigns against the Indians and Mexicans, not to mention his three years fighting Yankees during the recent War Between the States. Although he had been born in Pennsylvania, he had spent most of his life in Texas, where his family had immigrated when he was four years old. He considered himself a Texan; his memories of Pennsylvania were vague.

Although Russell was relatively young for his office, he had the fortitude to return his band of Rangers safely to Texas. For the moment, however, he was tired. The ride across the great Llano Estacado into New Mexico had brought out the worst in this Ranger unit. Russell was especially exasperated with Calhoun and McNally; he wondered why his superiors in Austin had saddled him with those two indolent soldiers.

Calhoun was the worst of the lot, but Russell did not have any choice but to tolerate this brutality. Calhoun was the son of a wealthy Waco rancher; his family was said to be distantly related to the former fire-eating senator from South Carolina who shared the family's name. Calhoun's father was a southern slaveholder and cotton grower with rich cattle investments throughout Texas. He had demanded his son spend some "maturing" time as a Texas Ranger, despite Calhoun's propensity for breaking, rather than upholding, the law.

As luck would have it, Russell thought, the bastard

44

fell under my command. Calhoun had a strong personality, and his influence on the Ranger unit was almost as strong as Russell's. *Which is why I let them take the Mexican girl,* he thought. *If the Comanches don't kill me before we get back to Texas, Calhoun might.*

For almost a month, Russell and his Texas Rangers had tracked that black horse thief Bill Bartlett up from Waco to the Trinity River and into the settlement of Dallas. Russell knew the real reason for pursuing Bartlett had less to do with horse thieving and more to do with allegations by the wife of a wealthy Waco rancher who had claimed "that nigger" had raped her. Russell had interviewed the woman and concluded she was probably lying to cover up a voluntary dalliance with the man. But the woman's husband and the local ranchers had demanded the man be brought back to Waco for a hanging. Russell had argued with his superiors in Austin that the Rangers had more important tasks than chasing after some horse thief. It was no use; the wealth and power of the ranchers had trumped Russell's pragmatism and logic.

In their pursuit of Bartlett, the Rangers had eventually moved north into unknown Comanche country. For several weeks, they followed the trail, crossing the panhandle not far from recent Comanche hostilities, where they suspected Bartlett might have taken refuge with the last band of Comanche holdouts. The trail, however, continued westward into New Mexico Territory. Russell had expected the locals would welcome his group with open arms or, at the very least, with the respect they deserved. He was mistaken.

New Mexico was not Texas. Russell found that in every village and hamlet they came to, the locals were mostly *mesicans*—and mostly uncooperative. Gringo raiders from Texas had terrorized the nuevomexicanos in the past, and distrust and suspicion lingered. The Tejanos were not welcome.

In the mountain range known to the locals as the Sangre de Cristo, Russell and his unit lost Bartlett's trail, owing largely to the rugged landscape. Unlike the shallow flatlands of Texas, the thickly forested mountains of pine, aspen, and piñon presented a challenge they could not surmount. Soon, they were discouraged, bewildered, and lost.

When they reached Santa Fe, Russell and his unit were again surprised at the numbers of Mexicans in the area. In the capital, Russell tried to obtain assistance from the local Anglo-American authorities, but he was advised to go back to Texas. "We don't have the resources to help you chase after some horse thief," he was told. "And we don't need you people running around New Mexico territory causing problems with our Mexicans." Although the Anglo-Americans in Santa Fe didn't say it—probably didn't even care—the "Mexicans" were technically United States citizens.

Russell surmised that a land grab was under way throughout the territory by Anglo-American interests centered in Santa Fe, and that they wanted things to go as smoothly as possible. "We have enough problems with these people as it is," one official told Russell, who recalled that a similar situation had been taking place in Texas for the last thirty years.

Russell had finally decided it was time to return to Texas. Then, two days out of Santa Fe, they had come across a small isolated farm occupied by local mesicans, as the men in his outfit referred to these people. Russell had intended only to water their horses and rest for a few hours.

Thanks to Calhoun, however, their respite had been cut short. Russell had made no move to interfere even when Calhoun and his cohorts had shot the boy and attacked the woman; the three were drunk and liable to shoot back, and Russell could not afford a gunfight in his own unit. When he saw Calhoun drag the girl from the house, however, he knew things had gone far enough.

Russell and Josiah Smith, the man they called "the preacher," rushed forward and pulled the semiconscious girl away. Calhoun pointed his revolver at her.

"All right!" Russell said, aiming his own gun at Calhoun. "Enough! You've had your fun."

"I'm just getting started!" Calhoun shouted back.

Russell raised the gun slightly. "Back away, J. D," he ordered.

Calhoun eyed the barrel of the gun and stared at Russell with fire in his eyes. He scanned his companions. Smith glanced at the sixth man in the group, Jason Allen, who was sober and perhaps no older than twenty.

"I saw a couple of horses over in those corrals," Smith said to Allen. "Go get one for the girl and bring it back here. She can come with us."

He then turned to Calhoun. "Will that satisfy you, J. D.?"

Calhoun grunted something that they took for a yes.

Russell turned to the others. "Ready your horses. Let's get out of here."

Now, a day and a half later, Russell found himself sitting beside a small campfire at dusk, somewhere east of the mountains in an area the Mexican natives called Las Sandías, chastising himself for letting Calhoun have the upper hand. *I'm a weak leader,* he thought, disappointed in himself.

He glanced to his right where Calhoun and a few of the others were already in their bedrolls. About five feet to his left lay the Mexican girl, her hands and legs bound. *If it were my choice, I'd cut her loose right now and send her back to her family,* he thought. *But it's not my choice . . . at least not yet.*

The girl was asleep, probably suffering from exhaustion and shock. It would be a long ride back into Texas. He had made certain that she ate and drank. He watched her as she slept. *She is beautiful,* he thought, *and strong.* At least he had managed to keep Calhoun and the others from having their way with her—so far. But it was only a matter of time before Calhoun again would be demanding his "entitlements."

Russell had ridden with men like Calhoun in the past. The men in the pseudomilitary outfit known as the Texas Rangers were supposed to be lawmen, but many of them routinely committed crimes themselves, raping and lynching Mexicans in the lower Río Grande Valley and South Texas. The powerful Texas ranching interests had always encouraged the Rangers in this, to "keep the Mexicans in line." Russell despised men such as Calhoun. *But he's what I have to deal with,* he thought.

The adobe house was silent. Joseph, the children, and old Señora Tafoya, were asleep in the large central room that served as a combined kitchen, living area, and children's sleeping quarters. Mateo remained in the alcove where María and Antonio normally slept. María dozed in her chair next to Mateo. Only Antonio was wide awake.

Finally, he grabbed a blanket and went outside into the cool night air. He sat down on a wooden bench perched under protruding vigas, listening quietly to the sounds of the evening. Crickets chirped from one direction; bullfrogs croaked among the cottonwoods near the creek.

Antonio stared at the clear night sky with its multitude of glistening stars shining like so many diamonds. He thought of Elena. *Where is she now?* he wondered. She was out there somewhere, probably on the llano under these same night skies.

Why am I waiting here for Eugenio to return? Antonio thought. *Certainly Eugenio would do everything he could to convince the authorities to help. But that will take time . . . and Elena does not have time.*

Antonio's heart ached for his daughter, and at the same time simmered with fury at the gringos who now held her captive. What kind of animals could such men be? Antonio finally realized that without sleep, he would soon be no good to anyone, least of all his daughter. He closed his eyes and allowed his emotional exhaustion to turn into troubled sleep.

Memories of Atrisco flooded his dreams. A vision of his grandfather Donaciano came into view. He could see the old man now, sitting by a small kiva-shaped adobe fireplace in one corner of the jacal. Donaciano was speaking of the old days, of youth in the Río Abajo. Antonio and his siblings sat on the floor, listening intently.

"My Tío was alcalde mayor of Tomé in those days," Donaciano said. "Although we lived here in Atrisco, Los Bacas also lived in Belén and Tomé."

"How many years ago?" Antonio's father Francisco asked as he rolled himself a cigarrillo of locally grown tobacco.

"Fifty years ago," the old man said. "I think the year was 1776 or 1777. I can't remember exactly," he said, shaking his head slowly. "So many years have passed. Yet, it seems like only yesterday I was sent to Tomé to work for my Tío Ignacio on his hacienda."

Francisco smiled wryly, "Tío Ignacio . . . el rico."

"He was a wealthy man; that's true. He was shrewd when it came to money and land. He had accumulated his large hacienda and holdings in Tomé."

"I wish some of that wealth had come to us," Francisco said.

"Wealth often has its price," Donaciano said. He paused and then continued. "For many years, beginning even before my grandfather's time, the Comanches had raided the Río Abajo, burning, pillaging, and stealing horses, sheep, and cattle. The Comanche raids had devastated that part of New Mexico.

"The people were always on the defensive, and constantly at war. Tío Ignacio Baca had tired of the deaths among his people and the losses to his herds. So, because Tío Ignacio was a prudent man, he managed to negotiate a truce with the Comanches and even befriended their fearsome cacique."

"Los Comanches," Francisco spat with contempt.

"No," Donaciano said. "The Comanches are just like you and me. They only want to feed their families and take care of their own. They are the horse people. This is their way of life. For almost ten years during the peace between Tío Ignacio and the cacique, the Comanches would ride down from of the llano once a year, through the Sandías and Manzano Mountains into the Río Abajo to trade and barter peacefully with the families of Tomé. We had peace for so long we had forgotten what war was like. The Comanches continued raiding the other villages of the Río Abajo, such as Alburquerque and the Pueblo of Sandia, but Tomé remained peaceful."

"Why did the peace last for so long?" Antonio asked.

"Because of mi prima María."

"Su prima, abuelo?" Antonio was confused at the thought of his old grandfather having had a young cousin.

"Well, my grandson, I was young once too, believe it or not. I was once as young as you. My cousin María was a beautiful girl with lovely eyes and a mischievous smile. She was full of life and energy, and the cacique desired her as a bride for his son. She and the son were both children, probably no more than nine or ten years old, when Tío Ignacio and the cacique made an arrangement that when María and the cacique's son came of age, they would marry one another."

Antonio's grandfather paused and sipped some wine from a tin cup before he continued. "Tío Ignacio negotiated this agreement in order to secure peace with the Comanches. For ten years, the cacique and his son waited, and the peace between the Comanches and the village of Tomé held." Donaciano stopped and closed his eyes, as he usually did when recalling the past. "So much time had passed that it seemed Tío Ignacio had forgotten about the agreement with the cacique."

"Had he really forgotten?" Antonio asked.

"Well . . ." the old man said. "One day, the cacique showed up in Tomé with his son, who had grown into a strong young Comanche warrior, to request the agreement be honored. They found Tío Ignacio and the village of Tomé in mourning. Tío Ignacio explained to the cacique that María had died of the pox only recently. He took the cacique and his son to María's grave.

"In reality, María had not died. Tío Ignacio had never had any intention of giving his daughter in marriage to the son of the cacique. She was actually hidden away farther south in Belén. The cacique and his son seemed heartbroken. They rode away from Tomé, declaring they would never return to a place of such tragedy."

Antonio's father nodded. "I would have done the same had I been the Comanche."

"Some time passed," Donaciano said. "María had returned to Tomé. Tío Ignacio was convinced he had saved his daughter from the Comanches. Then one day, during the mass for Santo Tomás, we heard a thundering noise. I ran outside with my primo and several others while Tío Ignacio and his wife and daughter remained inside. A cloud of moving dust approached Tomé from the east, the direction of the Sandía and Manzano Mountains. Then hundreds of Comanche warriors swept into the village of Tomé.

"The cacique, his son, and their Comanche warriors surrounded and then burst into the church where they killed poor Tío Ignacio and his wife in front of their daughter. They also struck down the padre and those in the congregation who tried to resist. I escaped, hiding behind an adobe wall while the church was ransacked and burned."

"And what about your prima?" Antonio asked in horrified fascination.

"Mi prima María Baca was taken by the Comanches. She was not seen or heard from again for years, not in Tomé nor anywhere else in the Río Abajo."

"What a tragedy," Antonio's father said.

"Yes, a tragedy, but one that was probably Tío Ignacio's own fault for trying to trick the Comanches. Someone in Tomé, or perhaps in Los Lunas or Isleta, must have informed the Comanches of Tío Ignacio's fraud, and the Comanches took revenge. However, some years later," Donaciano recalled, "I was on the Llano with a Cibolero party when we came upon a Comanche encampment. We were many hundreds of leagues to the east in La Comanchería, where the great Llano Estacado end and the endless prairies begin. We did some bartering with the Comanches. I recognized their leader as the son of the cacique from Tomé. I also recognized his wife. She was mi prima María, and she now had many children. She remained with the Comanches for the rest of her life."

She was not seen or heard from again . . .

Donaciano's words seemed to fade as Antonio awoke from his sleep and realized he had been dreaming. Donaciano was long dead, but his words now seemed to be a sign.

It was early morning but still very dark. Antonio arose stiffly from the wooden bench and walked slowly back into his house. Everyone was asleep.

Antonio slipped into the side room and put a hand on Mateo's forehead. The fever had subsided. Antonio

54

was filled with an overwhelming sense of relief. His son would live.

Antonio went back into the large room where the other children slept, along with the old curandera who had saved his son's life. For the first time in years, Antonio eyed the long steel Cibolero lance hanging on the wall. For many years, the lance had gone unused, for Antonio's days as a Cibolero were long since past.

He removed the Cibolero lance from the wall and held it with both hands. As he gripped it, he knew what he had to do. He could not wait for Eugenio to return, and could not trust in the authorities to rescue Elena. The laws of los americanos would shield the Tejanos but offer little protection to his daughter.

CHAPTER V

Elena's wrists were bound in front of her with a thin piece of rope. Her forearms ached, but she had enough freedom of movement to hold her horse's reins and guide it as the riders crossed the uneven landscape of tall grasses and brown, jagged mesas. She leaned forward in the saddle, trying not to look at the captors on either side of her. Two days had passed since her world had been turned upside down.

Several times she had considered giving the horse a strong kick and galloping away from these men, but she resisted the urge. There were too many of them, and she did not know if she could outrun their horses—or their guns.

The group moved slowly across the Llano. They did not seem to be in a hurry, nor concerned about anyone trying to stop them. She did not know where they were taking her, but they were headed east, toward the Llano Estacado.

Elena had heard some of the men utter the word "Texas" on several occasions. *Tejas? . . . Tejanos,* she thought. A shiver crept down her spine. She had heard the stories of the Tejanos and their cruelties toward la gente and los mexicanos. She was thankful they had not violated her yet, but she could sense from their glances that if the opportunity presented itself, they would not hesitate to take it.

She could still hear the gun firing at Mateo, followed by her mother's desperate screams. Were they dead? she wondered, blinking back tears. At least the younger children would be safe; Elena had managed to hide them in a narrow gap under the floorboards before the Texan burst into the adobe house.

Elena looked at the large man, the one they called "J. D.," and felt fury blending with her sorrow. Most of the group radiated contempt for her, her family, and her people; their faces were filled with disdain, not only for her, but also for the land about them. And this man was the most callous-looking of them all.

The apparent leader of this group of Texans, the man they called Russell, seemed different. His expression was more reluctant, as if somehow he was disturbed by what they had done. He had treated her reasonably kindly, feeding her when they stopped to rest and frequently offering her water from his canteen. *But if he's sorry about this,* she wondered, *and if he's the leader, why doesn't he just let me go?*

Although she had learned that Russell spoke some Spanish, she dared not trust him any more than she did the others. *I must be patient,* she thought. *The opportunity will come . . . I must have strength and patience.*

Antonio maneuvered his horse onto a trail leading out of el cañoncito de Los Bacas and into a wide river basin enclosed by a progression of red and brown sandstone bluffs. Through the valley flowed the clear blue waters of the Río Pecos. In addition to an assortment of shrubs and wildflowers, a series of tall cottonwood groves grew along the riverbanks. Except for an occasional ranchito and the ruins of an ancient adobe mission church, the area was largely deserted.

Antonio had left the ranchito at midmorning armed with a single pistol, a rifle, and his Cibolero spear. As the midday sun rose toward its apogee, its rays cast a blanket of stifling heat across the land. The sounds of birds and cicadas echoed through the canyon.

He was confident that Mateo and the ranch were in good hands. *Pepé will see to things.* Joseph had pleaded with Antonio to accompany him on his search for Elena, but Antonio had refused and said simply, "I need you to stay here and take care of the family while I'm gone." Joseph reluctantly agreed. Between Señora Tafoya, María, and Pepé, Antonio felt assured that Mateo would be nursed back to health.

A few hours earlier, in the cool morning air outside the adobe house, María had held her husband in her arms and said simply, "Find our daughter, Antonio."

"I will try."

"No!" she said sternly. Her voice cracked, overcome with emotion. "You *will* find her. Do you understand?" Her eyes were filled with tears. "Please . . . find mi hija. Whatever it takes, bring her home."

Antonio threw an old leather saddle onto his horse, mounted, and rode south through the canyon. He had packed only a canteen and a small cloth package of carne seca for provisions. The group of gringo raiders had a day and a half's lead on him, so he had to travel light to make up time. Antonio knew the Llano Estacado like his own home; if need be, he could find nourishment from the multitude of plants and animals.

Antonio's Cibolero lance, which he had hunted the buffalo with in his youth, hung from two leather straps attached to one side of the horse within easy reach of his hands. *Somehow,* he thought, *I doubt I'll be using the lance on any buffalo.* Riding out onto the vast llano without a Cibolero lance was not an option for Antonio. It was almost like an appendage to him, as necessary to survival on the llano as his arms and legs.

The Cibolero lance is life itself, he thought, recalling his first time on the llano. Antonio now saw in his mind his Tío Tomás.

When Antonio was ten years old, his father had finally relented and let the boy accompany Tomás out of Atrisco and onto the llano. The summer growing season and fall harvest in Atrisco, Alburquerque, and the surrounding communities of the Río Abajo had been meager that year. The carne seca obtained from the plentiful herds of buffalo that roamed the llano would see the family through the upcoming winter.

Although Francisco viewed the Ciboleros, with their nomadic way of life, as an unsettled and unpredictable lot, he was a practical man. Tomás could use the help, and Francisco's family could use the food. Although Tomás had always been too much of a free spirit for his brother's taste, having been involved with too many women and some minor trouble with the law, Francisco felt that Antonio would be in good hands. It might be good for the boy to leave the family for a month or two to see another land and another way of living. Probably Antonio would quickly tire of the Cibolero way of life and would realize his future lay in Atrisco.

Tomás and his nephew had ridden out from Atrisco on a cold morning in late September. The sky was gray and overcast. Clouds billowed over the rocky peaks of the towering Sandía and Manzano Mountains, like rapids gushing over a cliffside waterfall. Antonio was excited by the prospects awaiting him, but also apprehensive about leaving home for the first time.

They rode for many miles through the empty and silent *lamas* between la villa de Alburquerque and the Sandía Mountains, then into the narrow canyon of Tijeras, which separated the Sandias from the Manzano Mountains. An old trail rose through the canyon, eventually winding through a thick pine forest.

By nightfall, Tomás and Antonio had crossed the Sandias and emerged onto a vast plain of piñon trees, cacti, and shallow grasses. Antonio was overcome with a sense of wonder at the strange emptiness of this world. Further eastward lay the Llano Estacado. For the first time that Antonio could remember, he felt alone.

A large Cibolero caravan had set out to the llano from *la villa de Alburquerque* several days previously. Cibolero hunters from as far north as Taos and as far south as Chihuahua had converged on the Río Abajo to form a hunting party. The day before the caravan left the Río Abajo, the villagers at Alburquerque had celebrated with a mass and fiesta. The Cibolero caravan had included an assortment of horses, mules, and carretas, along with about a hundred men, women, and children. They would assist in the skinning, cutting, drying, and eventual packing of the buffalo meat before the return journey to the Río Abajo.

Francisco had asked his brother to stay behind the caravan for a few days, to help with the last of the chile and corn harvests. Tomás planned to catch up with the group somewhere to the east, at a place he called Bosque Redondo.

"We should have a good hunt this season," Tío Tomás told Antonio.

"How can you know this, Tío?" Antonio asked.

"I can *feel* it in this weather." Tomás' breath condensed in a cloud of fog. He smiled and added, "The sky, Antonio. Look at the sky."

The boy glanced upward. Gray clouds stretched to every horizon. A faint hint of yellow sunlight made a feeble attempt to break through. Although he was bundled warmly in his tanned antelope buckskin and leather clothing, Antonio shivered in the chilly air.

"Those clouds tell us snow is on the way," Tomás said. "That means the great buffalo herds are moving south."

"I don't understand."

"You will, in time. You have to look for the signs."

"How do I see these signs?"

"You won't necessarily see them with your eyes alone. You have to use all your senses, Antonio."

"I'm not sure what you mean."

"You'll find signs all around you, in the sensation of the weather or the shape of the land, or even in a fallen branch from the piñon, which can tell you men or beasts have recently passed by."

Tomás had told Antonio about the people of the llano, such as the Comanches and los llaneros—the latter being Jicarilla Apaches who often roamed the Llano Estacado, although not as far and wide as the Comanches. "Live like los llaneros or los Comanches, and you'll find the llano will be another home to you," Tomás had explained. "Like los indios, take only what you need from the llano.

The following day, Tomás and Antonio were still within sight of the eastern slopes of the Sandias and

Manzanos, though the mountains had dwindled to a mere shade of green on the western horizon. Antonio and his uncle had left the relative safety of the middle Río Grande Valley and ventured into the realm of los Comanches and el cibolo.

As the day wore on, the western mountain range faded completely from view and new landmarks appeared far ahead. "Do you see that?" Tomás asked, pointing toward a yellow-tinged plateau among a group of high mesas on the eastern horizon.

"Sí, Tío."

"La mesa rica," said Tomás. "Los pastores from San Miguel del Vado sometimes tend their sheep up there. The Comanches don't usually bother them on the mesa. It's too much trouble to ride up."

Antonio was beginning to appreciate the vastness of the llano and the life it offered.

"You'll come to know the llano in time," Tomás said. "But you have to be careful, especially in the beginning. You don't want to find yourself lost out there during a blizzard. You could freeze to death."

"Who lives in the llano?" Antonio asked, wondering if *anyone* could live in a land so vast and empty.

"Only los indios and our Ciboleros from Nuevo México. And perhaps a few Frenchmen from the north."

"Frenchmen?"

Tomás smiled. "Merely vagabonds. Our own people have been here since the days of el Conquistador Coronado." He paused and said thoughtfully, "It is said that Coronado planted estacas across the llano to help his party find their way in and out. But I don't believe it. He wouldn't have needed anything like that."

Tomás and Antonio spurred their horses to a faster gallop. They soon found the trail of the Cibolero caravan. By nightfall, they reached Bosque Redondo.

The Cibolero caravan from the Río Abajo was already there, as were two other caravans—one out of Taos and one from Santa Fe—and several groups of Pueblo Indians from Santo Domingo, Jemez, and San Ildefonso. Tomás was glad to see the *Puebleños,* whom he considered the best of the Ciboleros. The Indians' resourcefulness and efficiency would likely shorten the Ciboleros' time on the llano.

The Ciboleros had established a temporary encampment among the thick cottonwood groves of Bosque Redondo. Tomás explained that Bosque Redondo would serve as a base of operations from which the men would fan out and move up onto the llano in separate hunting bands. Some groups of Ciboleros would search for the buffalo herds around Aqua Corriente, Quitaque, and Palo Duro. Others would move farther east and follow the Río Colorado from New Mexico into the heart of the llano. Other Ciboleros would begin their hunt near the wild pastures and arroyos at Barrancos Amarillos. Still others would hunt farther south and east.

At the encampment at Bosque Redondo, Tomás arranged to stay in *el campo de Picurís.* He introduced

Antonio to Mañuel Archuleta, an old Indio friend from the pueblo of Picuris near Taos. Mañuel had arrived at Bosque Redondo two days earlier with his son Juanito. The Archuletas had set up a large tent to shelter themselves from the elements.

Antonio and Juanito were the same age and quickly became friends. Mañuel and Tomás set the boys to work gathering firewood and water. In preparation for the hunt, the men tended the horses and conferred with other Ciboleros.

While hauling firewood from the álamo grove near the Río Pecos, Antonio and Juanito stopped to marvel at a group of Ciboleros drilling their horses for the upcoming hunt. The Ciboleros were master horsemen, riding bareback and directing their horses at full gallop with their knees. These were an elite group, rivaled in skill only by the vaqueros of the ranchos and haciendas. The horses were trained specifically for running with the herds of buffalo, which sometimes numbered into the tens of thousands.

Many years ago . . . a lifetime ago, thought Antonio, as his thoughts returned to the present. Several markings on the ground had caught his attention. He reined in his horse and dismounted to study the earth.

Birds chirped nearby, and a small lizard scampered through a row of bushes. There was no one in sight, but the markings told him that men on horseback had recently passed this way.

Antonio bent to the ground and scrutinized the

horseshoe markings. It had not rained for several days, so the indentations were still fresh.

Seven riders, he thought. *Wait . . .* One set of horseshoes had left familiar and distinctive tracks. *My old work horse,* the one he had found missing from the corral when he had returned from Las Vegas the previous day. *Now the horse carries Elena.*

Antonio felt his heart pick up speed. He sprang back onto his horse and spurred the animal forward into the vast Llano Estacado.

CHAPTER VI

J. D. Calhoun was not a happy man. His brow was creased with furrows, and his mouth was turned down in a grimace. He sat beside the campfire next to his bedroll, chewing the last of the tobacco taken a month earlier from the lone Indian he had killed near Waco. As Captain Russell spoke, Preacher Smith and Private Allen stood watch nearby against the dangers of the night.

"We're not animals," Russell said. "We're civilized men."

"Then what is that girl good for?" Calhoun mumbled through his mouthful of chewing tobacco.

Russell frowned. "For profit," he said.

"How much is that madam in Dallas willing to pay us for the girl?" Calhoun asked skeptically.

"Depends on the condition she's in when the madam sees her."

"So, what are we talking about here, Captain?" McNally asked from beside his horse.

"If you and J. D. have your way with the girl now, you can forget about the money you could get for her in Dallas. She'd be damaged goods as far as the madam is concerned."

"She's a hell of a looker," McNally commented, glancing at the Mexican girl. The young woman sat on the ground on the opposite side of the campfire, her wrists bound with rope, her head bowed low. Although she did not fully understand the dialect of her captors, she sensed the general subject of their discussion.

Sitting next to McNally, Kyle Adams glanced from Calhoun to the captain, as if determining which man to trust and follow. "I'm sure she'd fetch a high dollar."

"I'm only looking after your interests," Russell said. "How much pay do you think you're gonna end up with when this is all over and you're back in Austin?"

"A pig's shit portion," Calhoun spat.

"Exactly," Russell agreed. "So doesn't it make some sense to get something for your trouble?"

"Damned right," Calhoun growled. "You do make sense, Captain."

"Okay, then we're all agreed here. Stick with my original suggestion. Keep the girl safe, and you'll collect your money in Dallas."

"Well, Captain," Calhoun said. "It sounds like a good plan you've got there, but it is unusual."

"How so?" Russell asked.

"Well, Captain, I'm not particularly fond of how you've been treating that mesican girl with a little too much concern . . . maybe even a bit of respect. Somehow it don't quite seem right in my eyes."

"That's not your concern, J. D.," Russell replied flatly.

Calhoun said, "I'm just trying to let you know, it seems to me you're showing just a little too much respect for that mesican girl. Where I come from, we know how to treat these mesicans. You have to keep these people in line . . . ours don't dare misbehave, or if they do, it's nothing a good lynching won't handle now and then."

"If you want to get your money in Dallas, you have to forget it now."

"I'm just making an observation, that's all," Calhoun muttered.

"This is the last I'll hear of it." Russell said. He stood up and looked at each of the men in turn. "You men best be getting some sleep because we have a long day riding tomorrow."

A short time later, Russell sat alone, staring at the dying campfire, sipping coffee from a tin cup.

Smith, whom the others called "the preacher" because he was a Baptist lay minister known for his fiery sermons back home, walked up and sat down on the hard ground beside Russell. "I put Kyle and Jason out on watch," Smith whispered.

Russell nodded. "Good."

"You reckon you know where we're at?" The preacher squinted into the flame as he lit a cheroot.

"We're headed southeast," said Russell.

Smith gently tossed a few dry twigs into the campfire and said, "I can't tell where we're headed. I lost my bearings yesterday when we got out of sight of those western mountain ranges. But you know best. I suppose we could have gone north toward Las Vegas after we left that ranch." He shrugged, obviously disappointed. He said, "Las Vegas might have given us a chance to rest in some respectable quarters. Maybe get cleaned up."

"No. We should try to stay away from these New Mexican villages and towns. I don't want to bring any attention to ourselves in these parts, particularly with our guest." Russell glanced at the girl, who lay watching them in the shadows nearby.

Smith cleared his throat. "Our guest or our captive?"

"Where we're headed, I suppose it may not matter."

"And where *are* we headed?"

"There's too much damned land out there to be certain. I suppose if we just keep moving in a southeasterly direction we'll eventually run into a Texas settlement."

"I didn't think we'd make it this far into New Mexico territory to begin with. Not after that land in the panhandle." The preacher took off his hat and ran his fingers through his sparse hair.

Russell shook his head slowly. "We'll be fine. As long as we can avoid trouble with any Indians, there's no reason we won't make it back to Texas safely."

"Crossing that llano damn near killed us and brought out the worst in J. D.," the preacher said.

"We can cross it again," Russell insisted. "I'll get you home, one way or the other."

"What about that thorn in our side?" Smith, whispered, glancing over his shoulder at Calhoun, who was already asleep and snoring.

"It's under control."

The preacher grunted. "He's a hard one to control."

"That's the kind of rabble I have to deal with."

Smith nodded. "Understood." He paused and pointing at the girl. "What happens with the greaser girl?"

"For the time being, she'll ride with us. We can't just leave her with these locals. We have no jurisdiction here in New Mexico."

"We're Texas Rangers," Smith spat. "We don't need *any* jurisdiction."

"The problem with you, Preacher, is you don't take circumstances into account."

"I don't follow you."

"This isn't Texas," said Russell. "This Mexican girl is a witness to a crime."

"Crime? What crime? I don't follow you."

"That boy was shot back there on that farm. I don't know if he's alive or dead."

Preacher Smith raised an eyebrow. "Killing a greaser ain't no crime."

"It is as far as a lot of the New Mexicans are concerned. For the time being, the girl goes with us."

"How far do you expect to take her?" the preacher asked.

"That depends."

"How so?"

"I suppose on how long J. D. and McNally ride with us."

"I'm surprised they haven't touched the girl yet."

"We've been riding the last day or so. There hasn't been much opportunity for them to take liberties. And I think I've bought some time."

"Oh?" Smith sounded surprised.

"I suggested to J. D. and McNally there's a profit in taking the girl back to Texas with us."

Smith shrugged. "I'm not sure what you mean."

"I told them they can sell the girl to a whorehouse down in Dallas, but if she's violated between now and then, she'll lose her value."

"*Do* you intend to sell her in Dallas?"

"Hell, no. But that's just between you and me."

Smith chewed his lower lip. "You know, any other Ranger captain would have let those men have their way with that girl."

"Look, you've got to side with me on this one. I know how you feel about the Mexicans and the coloreds, but if we're going to get back to Texas in one piece, you'll have to put all bad feelings away for the time being. You know the dangers out there. I need every last man, even a son of a bitch like J. D. I let them take the girl along because if there'd been a real argument, somebody might have gotten killed."

"I understand that. I'm not objecting to your command decision. You've just got to be careful with the likes of J. D." Smith paused. "All right, I'm with you."

"Much obliged."

"I just want to get home to my family and my congregation."

"We all want to get home," Russell said. "We should have been back weeks ago."

"We lost too much time looking for that horse thief. Too many greasers and papists in this New Mexico territory for my comfort," the preacher groused.

"Don't worry. Tomorrow morning we'll be off at dawn. Soon we'll get back to Texas."

"Amen to that," Smith said in a strong drawl. "Amen, indeed."

Many years earlier, young Antonio and his new friend Juanito had stood beside their horses at the edge of a broad ridge. They were looking down on a bowl-shaped valley formed from the rugged landscape of the llano, several days' ride from the Cibolero encampment at Bosque Redondo. For three days they had tracked a promising herd of *cibolos*.

Nearby, Tomás and the other horsemen dismounted to say a short prayer. Although Tío Tomás was generally skeptical of religion, he continued the Cibolero habit of praying before a hunt. When they had finished their ritual, Tomás and the other men again mounted their horses.

"You two stay here," Tomás commanded the boys as he planted himself firmly on his saddle and adjusted his leather trousers and jacket. The feather in the crown of his straw hat quivered in the early morning breeze.

Antonio responded, "Sí, Tío." He was apprehensive, sensing that great danger lurked within the herd of buffalo ahead. Antonio and Juanito watched as Tío Tomás, Mañuel, and three other Ciboleros continued on horseback into the valley. Each rider gripped a Cibolero metal lance.

Immediately ahead, at the center of the valley, the herd of cibolos grazed. These wild *vacas* of the Llano Estacado were unlike anything Antonio had ever imagined. The animals were large and stocky, with fierce hairy heads and thick brown legs. Hundreds of thousands blanketed the ground. They formed a vast dark shadow that stretched unimpeded toward the eastern horizon and the uninhabited lands beyond. The strong scent of bison dung hung in the air as the herd slowly made its way across the valley, beneath a red sky peppered with dark clouds that hinted at an early winter storm. The buffalo appeared oblivious to the approaching riders.

Antonio looked toward the heavens and felt over-powered by the sky. From this position on the llano, the sky seemed overpowering, barely an arm's length away.

Antonio shivered in the cool morning air. "How many are there?"

"Too many to count," said Juanito.

"They look like a huge black river!"

Juanito smiled. "This is a small herd. There are much larger groups out there." He pointed at the eastern horizon.

"What's out there?" Antonio asked.

"An endless country, filled only with los indios and los cibolos."

"But you are Indio," Antonio commented.

"We are from the pueblos, not the llano."

"Then there are Llaneros?" Antonio whispered.

"Comanches."

"And others?"

"Yes, there are others," Juanito said. "Foreigners from the East."

"Have you met such people?"

"At the Taos Fair," Juanito said. "There seem to be more of them every year."

Antonio had recalled seeing such foreigners occasionally in la villa de Alburquerque. His father referred to them as "gringos" or "bolillos." They were strange, hairy people, with fair skin and light hair, and they spoke a language he did not understand.

Antonio glanced west as Tomás spurred his horse into a gallop, gradually raising his lance above his shoulders. The horsemen were preparing for a run at the herd.

"This is my third year on the hunt," Juanito commented. "Last year's hunt was poor. We started too late and missed the larger herds."

"Larger herds?"

"The big ones that wander from the plains farther north."

Below, the party of Cibolero hunters abruptly dashed forward. One lance, followed by another, suddenly twisted in the air and pierced one particularly large bull. For a second, the animal merely appeared startled; then it moaned and stumbled.

As if suddenly aware they could be next, the entire herd seemed to move away simultaneously from the injured animal.

Tomás galloped forward and jerked the long Cibolero lance out of the bull's shoulder. Adrenaline pulsed through his veins as he skillfully speared the animal a second time. Mañuel did the same with his own lance. The animal struggled to run. The blows continued.

Soon, the bull collapsed to the ground. Antonio saw its sides heaving for a minute; then it lay motionless. One of the Ciboleros leaped off his horse, raced to the fallen animal, and slit its throat. A torrent of blood gushed onto the grass-covered plain.

Mañuel, Tomás, and the other Ciboleros dashed through the herd, working to spear as many buffalo as possible before the stampeding animals got too far away. Soon, the herd had disappeared to the east, and Tomás waved at Antonio and Juanito.

"Aquí!" Tomás yelled.

Antonio and Juanito mounted their horses and rode into the valley to assist Tomás, Mañuel, and the other hunters with the twenty or so dead buffalo now lying on the ground. The rest of the herd had vanished over the horizon.

Tomás showed Antonio how to skin and butcher a fallen bison, gripping a knife tightly to tear and pull the hide from the animal. For a moment, Antonio was repulsed at the layers of bloody muscles and organs, although it wasn't that different from helping his father butcher sheep in Atrisco. The buffalo skins would be cured and the meat salted and dried for carne seca, enough to feed entire villages during the winter; the excess would be taken south by caravan for sale in Chihuahua and Mexico City.

"We use it all," Tomás explained to Antonio. "Don't let anything go to waste. All parts are useful: the hide; the tongue; the meat . . . todo. And remember, when you hunt, you only take what you need. Don't kill more cíbolos than necessary."

Antonio nodded. "Sí, Tío."

Mañuel seemed pleased. "This was a fine corrida," he said.

Tomás nodded. "A few more runs like this, and we'll have a good winter ahead."

"But the herd is gone." Antonio pointed at the empty valley.

"Not far," Tomás said. "We can catch up tomorrow."

"It is moving east," Mañuel said.

"And these are not the only buffalo," Tomás commented. "There are other herds, further west near the Palo Duro and over at Agua Corrienta and Quitaque."

The names meant little to Antonio, mere words in the talk among the Cibolero hunters.

A cart, followed by three other carretas drawn by oxen, appeared on the western horizon. The men and women in the carts were the *agregados* who would finish the slicing and cutting of the meat. They had come from Bosque Redondo and would eventually return to their villages in northern New Mexico for the winter.

"They'll help us get this carne to the salt beds west of here for salting and drying."

"And then?" asked Antonio."

And then we hunt again," Tomás said confidently.

At that moment, Antonio had thought his uncle was the bravest man in the world. He had made up his mind to follow in his uncle's footsteps. Life in the llano was difficult and precarious, yet rewarding. *Some day I will be a Cibolero,* Antonio had told himself. *Someday I will hunt as a man on the llano.*

CHAPTER VII

A sense of regret, coupled with a nagging sense of shame, hung over Captain Travis Russell's head. He had had such feelings before, mostly during the recent War Between the States and during his time as a Ranger in the lower Río Grande Valley of Texas.

Unlike many of his fellow Texans, Russell had

never been able to view the Mexicans and Indians as animals or savages. But he rarely dared speak his thoughts aloud. Russell had always felt a bit out of place in Texas, even though he had lived there most of his life. His parents had been Quakers, and Quakers were pacifists, not to mention abolitionists opposed to the "peculiar institution" of slavery. When the family had first settled in Texas, back when the area was still a province of México, they had found themselves outsiders in a community of slaveholders.

While Russell's parents had joined the Catholic Church as a condition of their Mexican citizenship and small land grant, their conversion was only on paper. They continued to practice their Quaker beliefs in private. Still, they had taken their oath of allegiance to the Republic of México seriously; when war came, the Russells remained loyal. So after the Republic of Texas won its independence, and after Travis Russell's father had spoken too publicly against the increasing numbers of slaves in Texas—a stand which eventually provoked other Anglo-American "Texicans" to burn their farm and crops—the family had fled their small farm near Austin and resettled in an isolated part of south Texas. There, near Corpus Christi, Travis had spent most of his boyhood.

His parents' pacifist beliefs hadn't kept him from joining the Texas Rangers and, during the War Between the States, accompanying a Confederate column out of Texas into New Mexico. They were eventually defeated at Glorieta Pass near Santa Fe.

What bothered Russell most was not going to war, but that among the men he commanded were a number of soldiers who delighted in abusing the natives. They scalped captured Comanches, even children, and lynched Mexicans with no hint of guilt—even with enjoyment.

Russell despised such men. He had complained several times to the authorities in Austin that such men should be expelled from the Rangers. But no one else seemed to care; Russell suspected the authorities even encouraged such behavior. A number of wealthy South Texas ranchers, greedy for land, went so far as to offer fifty dollars for every pair of Mexican ears brought to them. Rich and influential, they feared no reprisal from authorities.

Russell had eventually given up any open protest against such brutality. *Sometimes you have to do what you have to do,* he told himself.

Now, on the harsh landscape of the Llano Estacado, Russell was the only Ranger not asleep or on watch. He glanced at the girl. Her eyes were still open, watching him. Perhaps the time was right to try talking to her.

Russell slipped over and knelt beside her. She looked at him with frightened eyes.

He placed his index finger to his lips, signaling her to remain quiet, then gently removed the gag. "Me comprende?" he whispered. "Do you understand me?" She did not respond.

"Mi español es pobre," he told her.

She remained quiet.

"I am not sure how to say this in Spanish. . . ." he said awkwardly. He paused and then said simply, "But I want to apologize to you."

Her eyes opened wide with surprise. Russell sensed she understood what he was telling her. "Habla inglés?" he asked softly.

Although Elena did speak English, learned in the boarding school in Santa Fe, she did not respond. If her captors remained under the impression that she did not understand what they were saying, they might reveal something that could help her escape. There was no sense compromising the tiny advantage she had.

Still, she instinctively felt that this man was different from the others. And any possible ally would be welcome. . . .

He reached out his hand toward her. She shrank back.

"Don't worry," he said. "I'm not going to hurt you. My name is Russell. What is your name?"

A sense of helplessness overwhelmed Elena. She had tried from the beginning to hold herself together, to not reveal any weaknesses to her captors. Now she could not, however, keep a tear from rolling down her cheek. "Elena," she said softly.

"Then you understand what I'm telling you?" he asked.

Finally, she nodded her head and said, "Un poquito inglés."

He sighed with relief. "I can't help you now," he explained. "I have to do all I can to keep this group together until we get back to Texas. Does this make sense to you?"

Again, she nodded.

Russell tied the gag back over her mouth. "I'm sorry to have to do this to you," he said. "Half of these men are out of control; there's no telling what might happen if they got angry. Just stay quiet and patient. In about a week we'll be out of this desert and into Texas. I'll be freer to act then. I'll find a way of getting you back to your family, even if I have to bring you back myself." Russell stood up and walked to the campfire and his bedroll.

Neither of them noticed the shadow crouched behind the large mesquite bush a few yards away. J. D. Calhoun scowled. *So the captain is a greaser lover.* Calhoun returned to his watch, silently promising himself that when the time was right, he'd make sure that neither the captain nor the Mexican girl returned to Texas alive.

Some fifty miles to the west, in the barren hills of the Río Pecos east of the Sandias and Manzanos, Antonio Baca stared into the star-filled night sky and wondered how his life had come to this. How had he allowed his daughter to be taken from him by the gringo strangers from the east. He gazed upward at the bright moon and wondered if his daughter could see the same moon this evening. *Hold on, my hijita . . . be strong.*

The llano called to Antonio as he wandered across the open countryside, following the telltale signs in the dirt of a party of horsemen. As the day progressed from morning to afternoon and the hot sun beat down upon his head, he felt he was making progress. He found a campfire and saw the fresh, soft outlines of her leather shoes etched into the ground, which indicated she was still alive. As the evening wore on, however, he realized both he and his horse must stop to rest, at least for a few hours.

Antonio suspected Elena was being kept alive for a reason. He could only guess at the motives of the Tejano horsemen.

"Tejanos . . ." Antonio grumbled. For as long as he could remember, the name *Tejano* conjured up images of rape, murder, theft, and, above all, arrogance.

Antonio had his first brush with the Tejanos several years after his first foray onto the llano with his uncle. Tomás and Antonio had joined a party of traders from Alburquerque who ventured across the empty land between Texas and New Mexico, finally arriving weeks later at the Mexican town of San Antonio in Texas. It was during this journey to Texas that Antonio saw firsthand the system of slavery the Anglos had imported from the southern United States and observed the general contempt the foreigners in the Mexican lands of Texas held toward their Mexican hosts.

During the year when Tío Tomás was not hunting

buffalo, the remainder of his time was spent either helping his brother Francisco in Atrisco or freighting wagon loads of goods for Don Gregorio Chávez, a rico from Taos, from New Mexico down the Camino Real to Chihuahua. Chávez also annually took wagon-loads of goods from New Mexico for sale and bartering in St. Louis. While gringo traders moved west to Santa Fe, Chávez and his party headed eastward toward the territories of the United States.

One spring, Tomás had invited Antonio to join him for the journey to St. Louis. The party of merchants from Santa Fe, including Gregorio Chávez and his son Juan, had left in early April. More than seventy wagons moved steadily eastward with Tomás and Antonio at the head of the party.

The traders wound their way through the heavily wooded Pecos Valley east of the Sangre de Cristo Mountains to the eastern settlement of Las Vegas. The party moved slightly north from the village of Las Vegas and then eastward toward the Llano Estacado and the lands of Comanchería.

One evening, while camped on the banks of a small creek, a band of raiders attacked the merchants. At first, Antonio thought the attack was the work of the Comanches.

Tomás knew otherwise. At the top of his lungs, he shouted, "Tejanos!" when he first heard the gunshots. The thieves were white men, Anglo Texans from the newly formed Texas Republic farther south. From their long hair, overcoats, and unkempt beards, Tomás recognized the men as Texas Rangers. He managed to kill several of the raiders with his bow and arrow. The Tejanos fled, but not before killing some of the New Mexicans.

In St. Louis, Antonio first encountered the world of the Anglo-American foreigners. This was a rough frontier outpost. Tomás called the settlement *a zoquetoso* because the streets were so muddy and filthy it was difficult to ride a horse on them, let alone walk. The town was filled with the brisk energy of merchants, thieves, and immigrants, many of whom, as Antonio had heard, had set their sights on the lands of New Mexico. *These people seem obsessed with money,* he had observed. Antonio also noticed black slaves performing most of the backbreaking labor. He saw slaves whipped publicly, and was particularly taken aback by the brutality they suffered at the hands of their American owners.

Antonio discovered in St. Louis that he had a natural gift for language, and it was here that he learned and practiced English. Tío Tomás urged Antonio to practice his newly acquired language, particularly when encountering the American women. Tío Tomás had been amazed at how easily he had been able to coax American women in St. Louis into bed. "We have to court our women for months or years, and then, if we're lucky, we can marry them," Tomás told his nephew. "This is a different world," Tomás had explained, adding, "and one I am afraid we will have to deal with sooner or later."

· · ·

By his twentieth birthday, Antonio was spending an increasing amount of time following the Cibolero way of life. Tomás had become almost a second father to Antonio while continuing to teach him the ways of the Ciboleros.

One year, after returning early from a hunt, Antonio and Tomás encountered a party of soldiers from Santa Fe on the plains south of the great Palo Duro Canyon to the north. Antonio had assumed the soldiers were hunting llaneros or Comanches. The commander, named Juan Tafoya, informed them otherwise.

"We've received word that the Tejanos are sending a force to invade our land," Tafoya said.

Antonio was stunned. Tomás was also concerned.

Tafoya eyed Antonio and Tomás and asked, "Ciboleros?"

"Sí," said Tomás. "We could use your help. We need trackers."

Tomás nodded and said: "You have our help."

"Gracias," said Tafoya.

For several days, Antonio and Tomás had assisted the soldiers in tracking a large party of horsemen and carts westward from the llano. Finally, in eastern New Mexico near the land grant of Anton Chico, the soldiers surrounded and captured a large group of Anglos from Texas. The invaders, who appeared lost, hungry, and thirsty, surrendered without a struggle.

On questioning, the Anglos admitted that they had been sent by the "president" of the recently formed

Republic of Texas, a man named Lamar in the Republic's capital of Austin, to conquer New Mexico and incorporate its lands into the Republic. Lamar had thus hoped to capture the rich trade of the Santa Fe Trail. The party had left Austin weeks before, traveling through the harsh uninhabited lands of the Comanche. But the expedition soon became lost among the seemingly endless canyons, plains, and mesas of the Llano Estacado. Word of their intentions to conquer New Mexico had reached Santa Fe well ahead of them.

There was one man among the Texans who was a Mexican and not a gringo. His name was Navarro. He had been impressed into service by the Texans to assist in their conquest of New Mexico.

"I've seen how our people are treated in your Texas," Tío Tomás told Navarro. "I made a trip to San Antonio and eastern Texas several years ago, after the defeat of General Santa Ana. Your great land grants have been violated, your women raped, and your men murdered. How can you support such thievery and murder?"

"I'm only trying to survive in the new order in our land. There are too many of them and too few of us," said Navarro. "Yes, these americanos in Texas are a cruel and lazy people. But they are like the toad who enters the burrow of a rabbit and puffs up until the rabbit is driven out of his home. The gringos were invited into Texas by the Mexican authorities and then they turned on their hosts and drove them from the land." Navarro's voice cracked. "Mark my words; they'll do the same here in your Nuevo México if given the opportunity."

The Texas prisoners were taken to the village of La Cuesta and from there up the Río Pecos to the town of San Miguel del Bado. They would be imprisoned there while the Mexican authorities in Santa Fe decided what should be done with them. Antonio and Tomás were asked to accompany several soldiers to la capital.

In Santa Fe, Governor Mañuel Armijo arranged for the Ciboleros' lodging. Antonio and Tomás would stay at the large adobe hacienda of "Don" Juan Chávez, the son of the late Gregorio Chávez. The elder Chávez had been killed by Tejano raiders several years earlier on the far eastern edges of the Llano Estacado. Juan Chávez, who remembered the two Ciboleros from the ill-fated wagon journey east, had heard of their splendid tracking. Although Juan Chávez was a rico from the upper caste of New Mexican society, he was not haughty or arrogant as were many ricos. Antonio had always found Chávez to be likeable.

The home of Don Juan Chávez stood near the Palace of Governors, not far from the central plaza where the large flag of the Republic of México waved. That evening they feasted on flour tortillas, green chiles, and beans with the don and the governor. The four men sat about a large wooden table while an Indian servant girl served the supper. After the meal, Chávez poured each man a drink of rum in a tin cup and said simply "salud," making a toast to the capture of the Texan invaders.

When the salutations were finished, Chávez said, "These are troubled times. It seems that invaders are at our doorsteps," Chávez added looking at Tomás. "At the request of the authorities in Mexico City, I have recently visited the territories east of Missouri, the eastern states of the Atlantic seaboard, from New York to South Carolina."

"What are the gringos of the east like?" asked Antonio.

"Perhaps not much different from those in St. Louis. They can be coarse and rude and brutal. They are, however, an industrious people," said Chávez. "They build great cities and buildings that seem to rise into the sky. There is much to be admired in their world, and also much to be questioned. They talk of democracy and freedom and equality, but only a few reap the benefits of such ideals. There is also something disturbing about these people." Chávez stopped.

"Yes?" Tomás asked.

"Los americanos are driven by an insatiable greed to own everything and everyone. Of course, I would be a hypocrite if I told you I myself do not desire wealth, but these people seem to worship money above all else."

The rotund Governor Armijo belched, plainly enjoying his rum. "They can stay in the East as far as I'm concerned."

Chávez smiled. "Except for their traders and merchants?"

"Yes," Armijo said. "We can still trade with them, but that does not mean we can trust them."

"What do you intend to do with the prisoners?" Antonio asked the governor.

"We'll march them to Chihuahua and let our authorities there handle the situation. The foreigners came to invade, to turn our lands into another Texas."

"It's curious," remarked Antonio.

"Oh?" Chávez raised an eyebrow.

"I had a chance to talk to one of them, a Tejano Mexican by the name of Navarro."

"Yes, I've met with him also," said the governor. "He was brought to the Palace of Governors this morning." He folded his hands and leaned back in his chair. "Tell me, honestly, your impression of these people."

"It is my impression that the gringos from Texas believe God has given them a right to rule any land they see fit. They actually believe that El Reyno de Nuevo México forms a part of their Texas Empire." Chávez stood and reached for a scroll of paper on the table. He handed it to Armijo. "Open it," he said. "I got this from a gringo trader."

The governor rolled the paper open and spread it out on the table. Antonio leaned forward for a better view. The document was a fanciful map with "Greater Republic of Texas" emblazoned across the top in English. The western border of the "Texas" map encompassed Santa Fe, Belen, and many other towns and villages of New Mexico.

"Arrogance," the governor spat.

"Clearly," agreed Chávez. "But this demonstrates the intentions of these people."

"Navarro told us the gringos despise any language or religion other than their own," Antonio said.

"That is true," Chávez responded. "My own father and many others have died at the hands of the Texans." He added thoughtfully, "Poor New Mexico."

"How so?" asked Antonio.

"We are so far from God . . . and so close to Texas."

A few days later, the Texas prisoners were marched southward past Alburquerque, through the villages of Valencia and Los Lunas. Several died along the way from exhaustion or thirst. When the survivors reached the capital at Mexico City, they were imprisoned for a year before being returned to Texas. Antonio had pitied the men, even though they were invaders. Still, they had been treated more kindly than Mexican invaders of Texas would have been. In the years since, many a Mexican in Texas had been lynched without hesitation, merely for remaining on his own land when the Anglos wanted it.

His mind returning to the present, Antonio adjusted his straw hat against the sun's punishing heat and continued his determined search for his daughter.

Chapter VIII

Several days had passed since Russell's conversation with Elena. The party of Texans and their young New Mexican captive continued across the eastern New Mexico llano. A flock of geese flew overhead, and several hundred yards to the left, two deer plodded up the edge of a jagged mesa. The heart of the great Llano Estacado still lay ahead.

Elena, her hands again bound in front of her, rode beside Travis Russell at the rear of the group. She again contemplated an escape attempt, but knew that if she were caught, the Tejanos would show her no mercy. And she doubted that Russell would be able to help her, however much he wanted to.

Would help come from elsewhere? she wondered. Elena thought of her father. He was strong, clever, and determined, but could he do anything against these treacherous men?

Russell had ordered Calhoun to ride at the front of the group, expecting an argument. To the captain's surprise, Calhoun had taken up his position without a word.

Maybe Calhoun has finally resigned himself to our Ranger rules, Russell thought, but somehow doubted it. Russell had slept the last several nights with one eye partially open and his shotgun in his hands. He had told the others he wanted to be ready in case of a Comanche attack, but he was actually keeping his eye on the

Rangers under his command, Calhoun in particular. *I don't trust any of them completely,* Russell thought, *and Calhoun would slit my throat if given the chance.*

Russell was unfamiliar with this part of the llano. The mountains that the natives called the *Sandías* and *Manzanos* had long since faded below the western horizon. Russell's best guess was that they were somewhere south or east of the settlement at Santa Rosa, but he was not certain. The llano was disorienting, a vast unsettled range of plateaus, of grass-covered hills, and of deep fissures that the New Mexicans referred to as "cañones." The land of the llano was foreign and frightening to the Texans. Hundreds of mesas and buttes seemed to expand in every direction, rising in numerous imposing patterns against a gray sky in the east and a pink horizon in the west.

Directly above were crystal blue skies and white billowing clouds. *The sky is different here,* Russell thought, gazing upward. *Even the air is different than in Texas.* Russell stared at the seemingly empty llano. *So far from home,* he thought. *So far from all I know.*

He felt lonely and insignificant—and uneasy. For the past several hours, an odd sensation had been nagging at him, as if someone's eyes were focused on them from afar. He carefully scanned the surrounding hills and plateaus, squinting in the sunlight, but could see no signs of any other human presence in this region.

As Antonio continued alone across the Llano Estacado, his mind again drifted into the past. The years had clouded many a memory, but he could recall one particular buffalo hunt as if it had occurred just yesterday.

On a cold day in early September, Antonio had spent his twenty-third birthday on an open plain named *La Ceja*. The surrounding ridges formed a faint outline, arching like eyebrows. The New Mexicans had hunted this territory for generations.

Antonio sat on his horse, watching a herd of buffalo move across *La Ceja*. Juanito Archuleta, his old friend from their early Cibolero days, sat nearby, also observing the slowly moving herd.

"We should wait for the others," Juanito said.

"They may not arrive for hours," Antonio said. "We could lose the herd by that time." The hunting this year had been poor. Although Antonio and Juanito had become seasoned Cibolero hunters, they had begun late this year and had missed the larger herds, which had already moved eastward.

"It's just the two of us," Juanito insisted. "We could use more hands."

"Maybe we *should* wait," Antonio said.

Juanito's eyes followed the herd toward the eastern horizon. He paused, then shook his head. "No, my friend, you are right." He glanced down at his horse and snapped, "Ándale!"

Antonio spurred his own horse forward beside Juanito. Dust and grass scattered as the two Ciboleros raced forward, each gripping a spear in preparation for the attack.

"Allá!" Antonio yelled, pointing out several buffalo that had fallen behind the others. The herd picked up speed at their approach, then suddenly swung west, directly into the horses' path. The roar of ten thousand buffalo, trampling the llano beneath their hooves, filled the air.

Juanito charged straight into the herd, gripping his lance high in both hands, aiming for a large bull just ahead.

Just before the spear could find its mark, the bull came to a sharp halt and spun toward its attacker. Juanito's horse whinnied and bucked wildly, Juanito lost his balance and plunged to the ground, his own spear piercing his body as he landed. The rest of the herd thundered directly over him.

Antonio, crowded aside by the edge of the moving herd, was forced back toward the safety of the ridges that formed *La Ceja*. He could only watch helplessly as thousands of los cíbolos galloped past.

Antonio's mind returned to the present as he saw the ramshackle building of adobe and wood. The worn structure stood alone on a small hill near an outcropping of rock. Several old álamos grew nearby, shading the building. A few goats and pigs roamed in an adjacent gated area.

He tied his horse to a wooden post and banged on the hard wooden door. A moment later the door swung open.

"Hombre!" bellowed the gray-haired man who had

answered Antonio's knock. "Antonio! It's good to see you, my friend. It's been too long." The man grinned, gap-toothed, through a slight beard.

Antonio stepped into the building. A makeshift bar stood along one wall opposite several old tables and chairs. Antonio's host closed the door and slapped his guest on his back. "How long has it been?" asked Antonio with a weak smile.

"Too long," the man said. "Not since . . . let me think . . . not since our last rendezvous at Bosque Redondo."

"That was a tragic time," said Antonio.

"Yes it was," the man said. He gestured toward a wooden chair. "Aquí. Sientate."

"Gracias, Mañuel," Antonio said, sitting down at the nearest table.

Mañuel limped over to place a bottle of rum and several flour tortillas in front of his friend. He gripped the chair next to Antonio's and lowered himself into it.

"I see you still have your injury." Antonio observed.

"It has become worse as the years pass, but I manage."

"You are alone?" asked Antonio.

"The others are with the cattle. My brother returned to the villa several months ago. My wife died last year."

"I heard. I'm sorry I was not able to attend her funeral."

"Thank you, Antonio, but I understand. Los Lunas is far."

"And the Luna family?"

Mañuel shrugged his shoulders and poured some rum into a tin cup. "What can I say?" He handed the cup to Antonio. "Los americanos refuse to recognize the land grant."

"But their laws are supposed to honor the land grants."

"Their laws are only for *them,*" Mañuel spat.

"But you are a rico. Surely you have powers others do not."

"Even the ricos have limited power against the might and arrogance of the americanos." Mañuel Luna shook his head slowly. "Besides, Antonio, I don't understand the language or the laws of los americanos, and I'm too old to start learning now. And I am still a Cibolero at heart, never one for the settled life in Los Lunas. The llano is my home. I leave most of the struggles to the younger Lunas. Some are learning the americano ways. Perhaps my heirs will be able to hold onto at least some of our land."

"Perhaps," Antonio said. "If only old man Luna were still around. He would not have stood for such thievery."

Mañuel smiled. "My father would have fought the gringos with his life."

Mañuel's father, el Viejo Luna, had once had a great land grant that extended from the village of Los Lunas to east of the Manzano Mountains. El Viejo Luna had been born in the days of the Spanish Empire. Antonio remembered him as a strong man with dark wrinkled skin and a long white beard.

The original grant from the king of Spain to Los

Lunas had been so extensive that it took a month and a half to cross it. It was on the Luna land grant that el Viejo Luna had met his end.

Many years before, Antonio and Mañuel had accompanied old man Luna to the eastern edges of the land grant. Antonio had met Mañuel Luna during one of the Cibolero hunts with Tío Tomás, and since then had often done work for the Lunas while in Atrisco.

That day, during the ride across the Luna land grant, old man Luna, nearly seventy-five years old, had stopped to water his horse at a stream. He dismounted—and nearly stepped on a rattlesnake, which promptly bit him in the shin.

"You will be fine," Mañuel reassured his father, but they all knew better, especially old man Luna himself. The snakebite was deep, and all they could do was make a rudimentary cutting of the skin, not enough to stop the spread of the poison. Although the old man found the strength to ride back, he gave out on the plains east of the Manzano Mountains. They were still at least two day's ride from the nearest settlement. Luna pleaded with Mañuel and Antonio not to bury him there, so far from his home in Los Lunas.

"I want my body to lie in sight of the bosque," he whispered. "I don't want to remain out here. Do you understand?"

Antonio and Mañuel nodded.

"I'm not of the llano, like you two are," the old man

said. "I want to rest beside my parents and my grandparents and their fathers."

Mañuel's eyes were filled with tears. "You will live, Father. Don't talk like this."

"You're a good man, my son, but we all die. That is life, and my time has come."

When old man Luna died early the next morning, Mañuel and Antonio knew that the body could not survive the return trip to Los Lunas without special preservation. So that afternoon they went to the salt flats, at the eastern base of the Manzano Mountains, and packed the old man's body in salt as they routinely had done with the meat of fresh-killed buffalo. Two days later, back in Los Lunas, they laid the old man to rest near his home.

"Your father was a great man," Antonio said now. He took another sip of his rum.

Mañuel smiled. "He made the journey between Mexico City and Santa Fe many times, back in the days of the caravans."

"I remember the stories about your father. He was said to have had a woman in every village from Socorro to Chihuahua."

Mañuel's smile faded as he paused to pour himself some rum. "I know why you've come here," he said.

Antonio was surprised.

"Word reached us here at Puerto de Luna this morning. A rider from La Cuesta brought the news. I'm very sorry, my friend."

"They have my daughter," Antonio said.

"Is it true what I heard?"

"Yes. They were Tejanos."

Mañuel pursed his lips nervously. "Los Rinches?"

"It appears so."

"How many of them are there?"

"At least six. I've been following their tracks since La Cuesta."

"Cabrones," Mañuel muttered. "How far behind are you?"

"Maybe a half day. Could be more."

"They came through here?"

"Nearby," said Antonio. "But I think they might be lost. They've doubled over their tracks several times. They're heading east."

"And your daughter?"

"She's riding my horse. I recognize its tracks."

"And what are their intentions?"

"You know how the Tejanos treat mexicanas."

"Yes, I know," Mañuel said sadly. "I was in Mora when they attacked from the East."

"Yes," said Antonio, remembering the stories of the Texan raid on Mora, when the town was sacked and burned. Other Texans had attacked trading caravans heading eastward from Santa Fe toward Missouri. "I'm afraid for my Elena," he said.

Mañuel heaved a sigh. "Still, she is lucky to be alive. Dios is watching over her."

Antonio nodded weakly. "Yes," he said, struggling to cling to hope.

"It's been many years since you've ventured into the llano," said Mañuel. "The land is changing. The buffalo are very few now. The Comanches continue to fight, but the americanos are strong. The days of Comanchería are ending. It will only be a matter of time before the gringos consolidate their ownership of our lands."

"Everything changes, it seems. Even the Ciboleros are long gone."

"I would help you, old friend, but I'm afraid I would only slow you down." Mañuel rubbed his injured leg. He had received the injury years ago, during a Cibolero hunt.

"You *can* help me," Antonio said. "I came here to ask you for food and water. María packed enough for a number of days, but it is running low and I do not know how much longer I will be searching the llano."

"I will give you some carne seca and tortillas. And help yourself to the ojito out by the álamos. You'll find plenty of water there."

"Thank you, my friend."

"I wish there were more I could do. Los vaqueros will not return until this evening, maybe tomorrow morning. I'll tell them you need their help." Mañuel paused. Then he said bitterly, "Los gavachos . . ."

"Bandidos," Antonio said. "Los rinches."

"You must find them before they are too far into Texas. If these Tejanos manage to make it through the llano, your daughter may be lost to us forever."

Antonio sighed and stood from his chair. "Thank you for the rum."

Mañuel Luna rose and limped to the bar, where he prepared a small package of food for his old friend. "Buena suerte," he said, handing Antonio the package. "You will be in my prayers."

"Gracias."

Antonio walked outside to fill his canteen from the fresh waters of the nearby ojito. The sky above was gray. A cool breeze swirled about him, chilling him slightly as he scanned the eastern horizon. Soon, his horse watered and fed, he was out again among the wild grasses and brush of the llano, still following the horse tracks.

Chapter IX

Captain Russell saw the rickety wooden wagon in the distance as it struggled through a thicket of small cedar trees and over a range of small prickly green cactus. Even from far away, the old wood and the poor condition of its wheels were obvious. Russell thought the wagon had a somewhat military construction, which caused him to believe it was surplus, a likely remnant of the recent War Between the States.

Russell, Smith, and Calhoun had ridden ahead of their party an hour earlier when they saw the cloud of dust rising from the distant prairie. Russell had taken Calhoun along primarily to keep an eye on that troublemaker. It was too risky to leave Calhoun alone with the others for long. The Mexican girl had remained with the other three Rangers; Russell believed he had convinced them not to lay hands on her for the time being.

In the distance, the wagon slowed down and stopped momentarily, obscured slightly by several large dry bushes. The wagon then continued forward. Now, Russell led his men toward the oncoming wagon, wondering, *Is that who's been watching us?* He had not shared his suspicions of being followed with anyone else in the Ranger party. *If that wagon's after us, why would they move out into the open?*

"What are you thinking?" the preacher asked Russell.

"I'm not sure. Could just be travelers."

"Or red Injuns," Calhoun added. "Maybe a stolen wagon."

"Not *that* wagon," the preacher said.

Russell agreed. No Indian would risk traveling in a wagon so close to falling apart. Besides, it was too easy to spot.

As the riders drew close, they could see that half of the wagon was covered by a ragged tarp and that the rest of the original cover was bent in various places. It seemed strange that anyone would take a wagon into the vast Llano Estacado in such poor condition.

The wagon stopped and a figure moved inside the tarp, away from their clear view. Calhoun, at the head of the line, suddenly froze. "Son of a bitch!" he shouted, galloping toward the wagon.

"Slow down!" Russell shouted.

The preacher spurred his horse in Calhoun's direction. "Calhoun's worked up about something."

Calhoun reached the wagon, drew his gun, and aimed it at the figure inside. The other two could see only the shadow of the driver as they drew closer. "Come on out of there!" Calhoun shouted.

There was a moment of silence followed by a voice that said, "I don't want no trouble."

Russell pulled up on the other side of the wagon and jumped down, his own revolver at the ready. "We're Rangers. We want to talk to you. Come on out!"

"What kind of Rangers?"

"Texas."

"Leave me be," the voice shouted back.

"We can't do that," Russell said.

"I want to be left in peace. I don't have a quarrel with you people. Do you understand?"

The preacher raised his own gun and fired a single bullet into the air. "You'd best be getting out here now."

A moment's silence followed. Finally, a man poked his head from the tarp and stared at the three Texas lawmen.

"Well, I'll be," Calhoun spat viciously.

A black man in tattered clothes stepped down from the wagon. He held a revolver in one hand.

"What's your name, boy?" asked the preacher, nervously eyeing the revolver.

"Nathan," the man said, his face exhibiting a combination of fear and resolve.

"Are you from these parts?" Russell asked the man.

"No, sir."

"Where you from?"

"East Texas," he said. "Not far from Nacogdoches."

"You're a long way from home," said Russell.

"Ain't never been my home," Nathan said with a hint of bitterness.

The preacher smacked his lips. "So boy, was you a slave?"

"I was. But I'm a free man now."

Wondering if the man was alone, Russell eyed the wagon. "Where you headed?" he asked.

"Into New Mexico territory. Place called Freetown, southeastern part of the territory, I'm told. I'm not sure if I've entered the territory yet."

"You *are* in New Mexico territory," said Russell, glancing at the broad plateau to the east from which the wagon had evidently come. "You had any trouble this way?"

"What kind of trouble?"

"Indians? Mexicans?"

"None," Nathan said plainly.

"You alone?"

"I'm alone," he said.

The preacher studied the wagon. "You sure about that, boy?"

Calhoun had dismounted from his horse and was rummaging around in the wagon. He pulled out some forks and knives, and two books.

"A colored man that reads," Calhoun said venomously. "Where I come from, that's a dangerous thing."

"It's the Bible," Nathan answered. "Got to read the Lord's words."

The preacher smiled skeptically. "I've read the Bible many times, my friend. Never found nothing there that says a colored man should read."

Calhoun removed a fur blanket from the wagon. "Well, look what we have here. Prime buffalo hide," he said as he pulled the blanket from the wagon. The hide was marked with several red streaks in a fork-shaped pattern.

"Injun markings," the preacher commented. "It appears our boy has been trading with the Injuns."

Russell ignored them and asked Nathan, "Are you traveling alone?"

"Yes, sir. It's just me."

"You run into any Indians?"

"A few Comanches, about a week ago. That's all."

"Trading with a Comanche can get you a hanging," Calhoun interjected.

"Maybe in Texas," said Nathan, glancing nervously at the surrounding mesas. "If this is New Mexico territory, I've been told you can trade with the Indians here. The Mexicans have been doing so for generations."

"This ain't Mexico," Calhoun growled as he eyed the wagon with suspicion.

"Well, this ain't Texas either. So there ain't no law against my doing it here."

"So we got ourselves a lawyer here," Calhoun spat. "You got your nerve talking that way to a white man."

Nathan's revolver shook in his hand. "Listen, I just want to be on my way. I don't have any gripe with you people. Just leave me be so I can move on my way."

Russell sighed and looked at the wagon. "Where did you say you were headed?"

"Freetown, sir. Some like myself are moving there, trying to start a new life. My brother is a soldier out here in New Mexico. He told me about Freetown."

"All right, you can move on," said Russell.

Nathan let out his breath, lowered his gun, and turned toward his wagon. Then a single shot rang out, shattering the silence of the surrounding landscape. For several seconds the black man stood erect and motionless, and then his legs collapsed. His revolver thudded into the sandy ground as he crumpled, life-less, beside it.

Russell ran forward and bent over the fallen man. A patch of red blood stained Nathan's back. Turning the body over, Russell saw that the shot had gone clear through the man's heart. "Jesus Christ!" Russell spat.

The preacher whispered, "Don't take the Lord's name in vain."

"A man is dead," Russell said. "I think the Lord will forgive me."

Calhoun moved away from the wagon, a rifle in his hand and a smug grin on his face. "Did I get him?"

Russell exploded. "What kind of an animal are you?"

"*Animal?* What the hell has gotten into *you*, Captain?"

Russell aimed his pistol at Calhoun's head.

"Enough!" the preacher snapped. "It ain't a crime. You can't be too hard on J. D. for doing something that any God-fearing white man in his place would have done."

"It sure as hell *is* a crime," Russell snapped. "It's murder."

"There ain't a court in Texas that will convict me for what I did," Calhoun said. "If anything, they'd pin a medal on me."

For a moment there was silence. Then the preacher said, "Okay, Captain Russell. What's it going to be?"

Hatred boiled within Russell. Calhoun represented everything the captain despised—cruelty, brutality, and injustice. Yet Calhoun was the quintessential Texan and he, Captain Russell of the Texas Rangers, was an anomaly in the Texas society and power structure.

As Calhoun stood smirking, Russell realized this was not a time to let emotions take control of his actions. He had no real allies in this band of Texas Rangers, none who would stand by him in upholding fair treatment for a black man or a Mexican. The only advantage on his side was the authority granted to him by the State of Texas, and that authority came not from the state government, but from the ranching and cotton interests.

Russell looked once more at the dead man and then

glanced westward at the forbidding, foreign landscape of the land known as New Mexico. Its jagged hills and deep canyons stared oppressively back at him. He looked eastward toward the Texas border, somewhere a day or two beyond the horizon.

Russell turned back to Calhoun. "We move on." He paused and then added, "After you give this man a decent burial."

"I ain't gonna bury a colored man," Calhoun snarled. "You have no right to ask me to do something so low."

"You'll do what I say," Russell said plainly. "I'm in charge of this Ranger unit." He gripped his gun firmly. "Either you bury this man properly, or you'll find yourself up on charges for disobeying an order from a superior officer. I'll see you hanging from a rope in Waco, and your daddy won't get you out of this one."

Calhoun bit his lip and glared at Russell for an endless minute. "Okay," he said finally, and began digging a grave in the brown earth of the Llano Estacado.

CHAPTER X

Antonio Jose Baca had been twenty-five years old when he met his future wife María in Taos. From his first glimpse of her, he knew he wanted no other woman. She was eight years his junior, the daughter of Jesús Aguírre.

María's father owned a small trading post where villagers, Indians, and foreigners went to barter whiskey, buffalo robes, meat, jewelry, pottery, and many other handcrafted products and items. Aguírre's trading post functioned as a combined mercantile store, cantina, bar, and community-gathering place. On any day, a French trapper from Quebec, an americano mountain man, and an Apache or Pueblo Indian might be in the same room of the trading post.

Jesús Aguírre came from a family that had lived in the Taos area since the early 1600s. Most of the family had been murdered in the Pueblo Indian uprising of 1680, but the survivors had fled Taos and returned ten years later during *la reconquista* led by Don Diego de Vargas. Their descendants, including Jesús, continued to thrive and prosper in the area more than a century later.

Antonio's brother Felipe had previously married María's younger sister Petra. Felipe had fallen in love with the auburn-haired, green-eyed Petra at first sight during one of the Aguírre trading visits to Atrisco. Since Jesús had no sons, his six daughters helped him run his establishment. Felipe returned with the Aguírres to Taos and began working for Jesús at the trading post.

Antonio, meanwhile, continued to follow the Cibolero way of his life, even after Tío Tomás retired to Atrisco and began a life of farming and raising sheep and goats. The Mexicans were gradually losing the eastern lands of New Mexico to the Texans, and a nomadic life was becoming harder and harder to maintain. Antonio himself was beginning to feel the urge to marry and to leave the llano for the settled life followed by his father, grandfather, and great-grandfather. So when Felipe invited Antonio to come to Taos and work with him at the trading post, Antonio agreed and rode up from Atrisco, uncertain what exactly to expect.

Antonio had visited the village of Taos only once before, prior to the influx of gringo wanderers and self-styled *mountain men* from the East. He had heard that much had changed in recent years. With the end of Spanish rule, the Mexican government had opened its doors to trading with the foreigners, many of whom walked openly in the streets of Taos.

Antonio had arrived at the Aguírre trading post on a warm autumn afternoon. When he was introduced to María, there was an immediate mutual attraction. He was thin but muscular, his face gaunt but strong; María was vibrant and beautiful, with soft brown skin and innocent green eyes. She was only fifteen years old, but she already seemed a woman. After several weeks of courtship, it was announced that Antonio and María would soon be married.

Like most nuevomexicanos, Antonio had little formal education. He was, however, luckier than most of his compatriots. Although Antonio's father was illiterate, his mother could read and write, having learned from the nuns at the San Felipe de Nevi church in Alburquerque when she was a child. Antonio's mother taught him and his brothers the basics of reading and writing Spanish. Through his wanderings on the Llano Estacado and into the lands of the Tejanos and the americanos to the east, he had also learned to speak English.

Antonio had taken immediately to the business of running a trading post. While Jesús negotiated trading of hides, food, and dry goods, Antonio and Felipe had kept the small adobe trading post operating. The days were long and the nights short, but Antonio found ample opportunity to hone his reading and writing. He also practiced his English, conversing with the foreigners who frequented the trading post.

Jesús Aguírre's tiny adobe trading post had once served as a hostel. The one-story brown structure had stood on the plaza since the early 1600s and now included several storerooms, a long wooden bar, and several pieces of carved wooden furniture that had been crafted in *la capital,* Mexico City, and brought up the Camino Real to Taos by a caravan of oxen and mule.

In a short time, Antonio was well acquainted with the leading citizens of Taos, both native and foreign. Jesús introduced him to Padre Martinez, the well-respected priest of the Taos church; the French-Canadian trappers, Antoine and Abraham Ledoux, brothers who had made the long overland trip from Quebec to the Mexican province of Nuevo México; and several recently arrived interlopers. Not all of them were friendly. Two who particularly stood out were a man named Kit Carson and his associate, Charles Bent. Carson was a tall bearded man from the East. He spoke some Spanish and was married to María Josefa Jaramillo, the daughter of one of the leading New Mexican citizens of Taos. Antonio wondered how a rough and *feo* like Carson had managed to marry Josefa. *It must be some sort of marriage of convenience,* Antonio thought.

Bent had a wild beard and long blond hair, and he welcomed the hospitality and citizenship offered by México while looking on the locals with contempt. Bent strutted the streets of Taos as if anointed by God himself, one in a long line of swaggering mountain men who had wandered into the Taos area in recent years. The Mexican authorities in Santa Fe tolerated the obnoxious behavior by such men, hoping that an influx of American citizens would assist in maintaining and increasing trade with the United States.

Antonio, who had to deal with the foreigners every day, thought the government—and many of his fellow New Mexicans—were naïve, unable to see the obvious greed and avarice with which the newcomers looked upon the lands of New Mexico. Bent even condescendingly referred to the Mexicans of Taos as "my children."

One afternoon, Antonio overheard a conversation between Carson and Bent at the trading post.

"It's only a matter of time before war comes," Carson said, sipping from a wooden cup filled with beer. Antonio was refilling Bent's cup.

"Gracias," Bent said in Spanish, then turned to speak to Carson in English. "If there's one thing these people can do properly, it's make wine and beer." He grinned and added, "And their very own Taos Lightning."

Antonio returned to the bar. He continued to listen quietly as he busily wiped plates and glasses. Neither Carson nor Bent seemed concerned about whether Antonio could overhear them. Perhaps they didn't know he understood English. In any case, the beer had already gone to their heads and their mouths.

"There is opportunity to be had here. These people won't be able to hold onto this land when the army arrives," Brent said.

Carson smiled and swallowed more beer, letting the froth cake his scraggly light brown beard. "These people may not surrender as easily as you think. They may be ignorant and uncivilized, but they are fighters and hunters."

Bent smiled. "A few good scalpings should be enough to keep them in line."

"Like you've done to many an Injun," said Carson admirably.

"These Mexicans are like children." Bent laughed. "I know these people. I've lived among them. I've married one of their women. They need guidance and the white man's civilization. They'll make wonderful servants and fine sharecroppers once we bring civilization and the Lord's proper English to this wild land."

"All in good time, of course."

"There's money to be made here, Kit. There is land here for the taking."

"It may not be that easy."

"Why not? These people don't even understand or respect the concept of property. Look at these land grants. They share the land in common, supposedly for the good of all. What kind of a system is that? The Mexican race is a corrupt one. It's in their nature. They have few morals and can be swayed easily. If anyone should know that, it's *you*."

Carson raised an eyebrow. *"Me?"*

"You've managed to marry the daughter of one of the wealthiest men in Taos. *You,* of all people? Even with your squaw wife up north, your wife's father didn't object."

Carson tensed with sudden anger. "That's my business, Bent. Besides, Josefa is *your* sister-in-law. You're the one who talked me into taking a wife here. I followed your path."

"Of course, my friend, of course. My wife is a native, too. The women in these parts *are* beautiful, for certain. They make fine wives. But their men are lazy and shiftless. You can't trust 'em."

Bent paused, then smiled. "You've been a scout for the Union army. You surely *know* what I'm talking about. These Mexicans have invited the fox into the henhouse. They haven't a clue what awaits them once our army arrives."

Carson leaned back in his chair and placed his hands on the table. A hint of arrogance ran across his face. "Times are changing in New Mexico. That much is certain." He raised his cup and took another swallow of beer. "What have you heard from the East?"

"I was in St. Louis five months ago. They're already recruiting volunteers from Missouri. The word is out that land is here for the taking. I hear that Kearny will lead the advance team. The conflict with México is inevitable. President Polk just needs an excuse to justify a war. He'll find one sooner or later."

"Well, I hear that the Texans are trying to stir up a war down in the lower Río Grande Valley," said Carson. "They left México; now they want to join the United States." He sipped the last of his beer and glanced down the length of the long bar, on the other side of which stood Antonio, gently wiping a glass. Carson paused and then commented in a low voice, "We're talking treason, of course."

Bent smiled. "Treason to these greasy Mexicans? You have to be fooling me."

Carson glanced back at Antonio. "I think we've already said more than we should have."

"It's the beer talking," said Bent. "Beside, these people can hardly speak proper Spanish, let alone a superior language like English. Don't worry. That boy is just a servant. I'm sure he doesn't speak a word of English. He can't understand you.

Antonio was not about to let on that he did understand their language. He continued to clean dishes without looking up.

Bent raised his hand at Antonio and barked in Spanish—with a harsh Anglo-American accent— "Más cerveza." Antonio went to refill Bent's and Carson's cups.

As he walked back to the bar, he heard Bent say, "Our American comrades here in New Mexico are getting nervous, especially the Texans in Taos."

"Crazy people, those Texans." Carson grinned. "They've been itching to get their hands not only on New Mexico territory, but on all of the lands to the Pacific."

"You have to admire them," said Bent. "The Texans know how to treat these lower races—the Mexicans, the Indian savages, and especially the blacks. Maybe with Texans running this territory, these Mexicans will learn their place."

Antonio now rode slowly toward the lone wagon, motionless on the eastern horizon. Silence permeated the rugged landscape. The wagon seemed out of place in this isolated valley, surrounded by sharply rising mesas and by fields of tall brown and green grasses freshly watered from the recent rains.

Antonio recognized this valley from his days as a Cibolero. Hundreds of thousands of buffalo had once roamed this valley, moving in large herds from *El Reyno de Nuevo México* east of the Canadian River Canyon to the region the Americans labeled Indian Territory. He recalled many a successful buffalo hunt in this valley.

Antonio approached the wagon cautiously. He stopped and dismounted, then stood there listening for any sound. Hearing nothing except a soft wind blowing, he walked forward. A shallow mound near the wagon caught his eye. Stooping over it, he recognized the small hill as a freshly dug grave.

Then a faint sound from behind caught his attention. Antonio spun around. At first there was silence, then a noise like a muffled cry, from the direction of a boulder some twenty-five feet away.

Cautiously, Antonio walked back to his horse and removed his rifle from its saddle-mounted leather casing. Gripping the rifle in his hands, he crouched low and crept toward the boulder under the cover of large shrubs and outlying branches.

Antonio reached the boulder and stopped to listen again. At first he heard only the breeze rushing past him. Then the noise came again, from directly behind the boulder. Antonio cautiously followed the sound around the boulder. There he found the source of the noise.

Two terrified black children, a boy and a girl, crouched there, clinging to each other, fear etched on their faces. They were very young—clearly out of place, alone in this isolated valley of the Llano Estacado. Antonio stared at them. They appeared to be in a state of shock.

A snapping noise sounded behind. He turned to see a dark-skinned boy, perhaps thirteen or fourteen years old and probably the brother of the other two, with a large revolver aimed directly at Antonio's chest.

The boy said, "I'll be shooting you, mister."

Antonio raised his own gun and said, in English, "You don't want to do that."

"You killed my pa," said the boy.

"I only just arrived now."

"You're with them murderers."

Antonio was perplexed. "I don't know what you mean."

"You're with those white men," the boy insisted angrily.

Antonio shook his head slowly. "That is not so. Do I look white to you?"

The boy studied Antonio closely. "No, I reckon not. You a Mexican?"

Antonio nodded. "This is Nuevo México," he said.

"New Mexico. Yes, that's where we're headed."

Antonio took a deep breath. "I'm going to lower my rifle. Do you understand?"

The boy's eyes opened wide, filled with mistrust and uncertainty.

"I don't want to shoot you," said Antonio. "And I certainly do not want you to shoot me." He slowly placed the rifle on the ground, then stood up straight and opened his arms. "You can shoot me if you like, but I am telling you the truth. I am not with these men you say killed your father."

The boy looked at the rifle and then at his sister and brother. "No, I suppose you're not with those men. They were different from you. They weren't Mexican."

"Is your father buried back there?"

"Yes," the boy said, lowering his weapon.

"You have horses?"

117

"We had two horses, but those white men took one of them."

"After they killed your father?"

The boy nodded. "Yes." He explained, "My pa ordered us out of our wagon when he saw the white men coming. We stayed low and hid behind the bushes."

"Do you still have the other horse?"

"Yes," said the boy. "It's safe."

"Can it pull your wagon?"

"I think it's strong enough."

"Good," said Antonio. He went to the two younger children and said to them gently, "Niños, do not have fear. Follow me."

Antonio stooped to pick up his rifle and then led the three children away from the large boulder, back to the wagon. "Go bring your horse," he told the older boy, who vanished into the shrubs and quickly returned, leading the animal.

Antonio made a small campfire and offered the children some of his water and carne seca. A slight chill hung in the air, and while the children were plainly traumatized over the death of their father, they seemed somewhat reassured by the warmth of the fire.

"Where was your father taking you?" Antonio asked the oldest.

"Freetown."

Antonio nodded. "I have heard of that place. It is the settlement where the freed slaves live. But it is a long distance from here. You can't go there alone."

"We have no one else," said the boy. He paused and added, "Except our uncle. He's in the army in New Mexico territory."

"And your mother?"

"She died in Texas."

Antonio thoughtfully tossed a mixture of dried grass and twigs onto the fire. "You need to find the Buffalo Soldiers."

The boy stared blankly. "Buffalo?"

"The black americano soldiers, los indios call them the Buffalo Soldiers. You might find some of these soldiers at Fort Sumner, near the area we call Bosque Redondo. Go there. They can help you look for your uncle and Freetown."

"Can you take us there?" asked the boy.

Antonio was torn by the boy's request. "I wish I could, my young friend," he said sadly, "but I can't." He pointed to the horseshoe tracks in the surrounding earth. "A group of men—probably the same ones who killed your father, judging from these tracks— abducted my daughter several days ago. I have to catch up with them quickly, or they might kill her too."

The boy stared in silence for a few seconds. Then he said thoughtfully, "I wish I could help you."

"You can help me by going to Fort Sumner and finding your Buffalo Soldiers. Will you do that for me? Will you do that for your father?"

"Yes." The boy nodded.

Antonio went to his horse and placed his rifle back

into its sling. As he mounted, he turned once more to the three children. "Due west," he said. "It's a two-day ride directly west." Antonio eyed the horseshoe tracks, embedded like scratches in the earth. "Buena suerte. Good luck to you, my young friend. Vaya con dios."

CHAPTER XI

Antonio had married María in Taos on a warm Saturday afternoon in mid-August. It was a perfect day. The surrounding Sangre de Cristo Mountains rose sharply into the clear blue sky. Flocks of birds flew overhead among the dark green shadows of the nearby mountains. The wedding mass and ceremony were officiated by Padre Martinez in a small chapel near the Taos plaza.

A wedding fiesta was celebrated in the town plaza after the ceremony. The Alcalde of Taos and several other local magistrates enjoyed the festivities and the music of a small group of guitar and violin players. As the music played, the wedding guests ate, drank, and danced.

"It is a good day," his brother Felipe told Antonio, as they sipped wine from wooden cups.

"Indeed," said Antonio. A satisfied smile formed on his lips as he watched María and Petra giggling together a few feet away. *What are they discussing?* he wondered.

Felipe and Antonio stood beneath a large flagpole at the center of the plaza. A large green, white, and red flag with the outline of an eagle rippled above them in the gentle breeze. *México,* Antonio thought to himself. *Y Nuevo México.* The country of México itself had always been something of a distant image for New Mexicans. Although Mexican citizens, they felt less of a kinship with their fellow countrymen in the distant south than with the isolated village communities of New Mexico.

The brothers' father-in-law approached, slightly inebriated but quite happy. He patted Antonio on the back and said with a slight slur, "It's good to have another Baca in the family."

"Thank you, Jesús," Antonio said.

"You're good boys. Hard workers. We're lucky to have you."

"Would you like to sit down?" asked Antonio.

"No, my boy. I'm fine. I just want to tell both of you that you're like sons to me."

"You've been good to both of us," Felipe said.

Antonio nodded.

Jesús Aguírre said, "Más vino," and abruptly turned and went to rejoin the other partygoers.

Felipe helped himself to an olla of frijoles and warm tortillas sitting on a nearby wooden banquet table. "Will you stay in Taos, Antonio?"

"I would like to return to Atrisco to help our father."

"And the llano and the los Ciboleros?"

"I have not forgotten the llano," Antonio said. "Perhaps once in a while I may still hunt the buffalo."

"It is no life for a married man."

"That is true," said Antonio. "Still, I already miss the llano, like a sailor misses the sea."

"You have a wife now, Antonio. You can't be running off to the llano for weeks or months at a time."

Antonio recognized the truth of his brother's words. Their life and world were changing.

Antonio looked up at the flag of México and thought of the news that had reached Taos the previous day. American forces under the command of General Stephen Watts Kearny had entered Santa Fe unopposed through Apache Pass to the east. Governor Armijo had apparently left the pass undefended; rumor even suggested that the governor had left Santa Fe with a $50,000 payoff from General Kearny.

"What will become of us?" Felipe asked, as if reading his brother's thoughts.

"I don't know." Antonio scanned the surrounding mountains. "It seems the americanos want to seize everything, not only the land but also the people. They enslave the black people in the East for hard work. They came here as our guests and accepted our hospitality, even married our own women, and now they have betrayed us."

"I heard Carson and Bent are down in Santa Fe with the American army," said Felipe.

"I'm not surprised," said Antonio. "Not at all."

Another voice interrupted Antonio's and Felipe's conversation. "I could not help but overhear," said Padre Martinez. The round-faced, balding priest held a cup of wine in one hand and a sugar-coated *bisco-*

122

chito in the other. Antonio was amused; he rarely saw a priest sipping wine. *This is why I like Padre Martinez,* Antonio thought. *He is fully human, one of us.*

"We were discussing how the world is changing," said Felipe.

"It will no longer be the same. That is certain," said the priest.

"Do you trust the americanos?" asked Antonio.

Before the priest could answer, a distant sound rose above the music and chatter filling the plaza air. The noise drew closer until it became a steady, distinct beat. The music and chatter in the plaza fell silent.

The noise was now obviously the sound of a drum beating, intermixed with the neighing of horses and marching feet. Then a long row of soldiers in blue uniforms entered the plaza, stepping to the beat of the drum, followed by twenty mounted cavalrymen and a series of horse-drawn carts and cannons. A cloud of dust and dirt filled the air as the soldiers came to an abrupt stop near the edge of the plaza.

An officer barked orders. A detachment of five soldiers broke away from the column and pushed their way through the crowd of stunned wedding guests. Antonio saw one soldier shove an elderly gentleman away to make room for the commanding officer.

"Step aside!" the officer shouted at Antonio and Felipe, who moved away from the flagpole and stood protectively in front of their wives. A crowd of *Taoseños* who had not been at the wedding celebration were now gathering around the plaza.

Two of the American soldiers stepped up to the flag-pole and began lowering the Mexican flag. Another soldier, standing near the commanding officer, removed a red and white striped cloth from a flat leather pouch. Antonio recognized the national flag of the americanos.

The Mexican flag reached the ground. The American officer grabbed it with two hands, ripped it in half, and threw it to the ground in front of the startled crowd.

Then he scanned the Taoseños. "You there!" he yelled, pointing at Felipe. Felipe took an uneasy step backward.

Another soldier circled behind Felipe and poked the barrel of a rifle in his back. "Move your ass!" the solider bellowed. Felipe stood motionless, his face blank with shock.

"The captain is calling you," the soldier snarled. "Don't you understand English?" He pushed Felipe toward to the flagpole and the commanding officer.

The officer shoved the American flag into Felipe's hands. He then turned to face the crowd and yelled out, "I want this man, one of your people, to raise your new flag, the flag of the United States of America!"

Confusion and anger flashed across Felipe's face. For a moment he stood there, the Mexican flag lying torn at his feet, the red, white, and blue cloth clutched in his hands. Then he let the American flag drop into the dirt, next to the fallen flag of México.

Felipe squared his shoulders and looked the commanding officer directly in the eye. "No."

The soldier's face twisted into an expression of disbelief.

As Felipe turned to walk away, the butt of a soldier's rifle crashed against his head. He crumpled to the ground next to the flags, blood trickling down the side of his face.

Antonio ran to his brother, yelling "Cabrones!" Out of the corner of his eye, he saw the soldier raise the rifle for another blow. Padre Martinez leaped between Antonio and the soldier.

"Basta! Please! Enough!" Martinez shouted, using the little English he knew. He quickly turned to Antonio and said in Spanish, "I'll take care of your brother. Please, raise the new flag yourself, and then we will all leave."

Antonio realized he had no choice in the matter. As Padre Martinez and a man from the wedding guest carried Felipe away from the plaza, Petra ran after them, weeping. Antonio glanced at María and nodded for her to go with her sister.

"Pick up *your* flag," the commanding officer said. Antonio looked at the ground, surveying the two flags. With a heavy sigh and a broken heart, he stooped to pick up the American flag and proceeded to raise it up the flagpole.

When the flag reached the top of the pole, a drum rolled and a beaming smile formed on the commanding officer's face. The officer scanned the Taos plaza as if expecting to see faces filled with gratitude. Instead, a palpable cauldron of resentment simmered beneath a sea of outwardly humble eyes.

Calhoun cursed silently to himself as he maneuvered his horse onto a high ridge at dusk. The other Rangers had made camp about two miles to the west. Captain Russell had sent Calhoun and McNally ahead to forage for water and food. The band of Rangers was running low on both.

McNally spat tobacco. "That ain't right what the captain made you do . . . digging that grave."

"There's a lot of things the captain does that ain't right."

"Like the Mexican girl?"

"I've had my fill of the captain's promises."

"He said we'd all make a pretty penny off of it."

"That's if we make it back to Dallas," Calhoun grumbled. "How about another chaw of that tobacco?"

"I'm out," said McNally.

"Damn."

"Do you think the captain has gotten us lost, J. D.?"

"I don't know, but I have my doubts about the man."

The sun was slowly sinking on the western horizon, leaving darkness in its wake. McNally turned his head and peered into the distance.

"You see something?" Calhoun asked.

"I think so. It's over yonder that way. A light. Do you see it?"

"Yeah, I see it."

"What do you think it is?"

"Looks like a campfire," said Calhoun, urging his

horse in the direction of the flickering light. "Let's check it out."

McNally hesitated. "Captain told us to get right back if we can't find anything worth eating."

"No," said Calhoun. "I'm going to see what's there. You can stay here if you want."

"It's getting late."

"You do what you want."

McNally sighed and directed his horse after Calhoun's. The two clambered downward through a thicket of sagebrush and cactus. The moon was already rising in the night sky by the time they reached level ground, cast a glow across the silent countryside.

A faint campfire burned a few hundred yards away. The Rangers dismounted and tied their horses to a large, thorny bush. Calhoun pointed to another bush, closer to the campfire. They darted forward and crouched behind that shrub.

Now they could see a man sitting alone by the campfire. The man had his back to them, but he was obviously an Indian. *Maybe Comanche or Apache,* guessed Calhoun. No one else was in sight.

Calhoun sensed an opportunity and pointed to a leather pouch on the ground, a few feet from the Indian. "Look yonder," he whispered. "See that pouch?"

McNally nodded, peering into the darkness. "Yeah, I see it."

"Likely water," said Calhoun.

"Yeah. I reckon so," McNally said softly.

"Seems that Injun has plenty to drink and eat."

"What do you have in mind?"

Calhoun pulled out a large Bowie knife and showed it to McNally. The wide blade glinted in the moonlight.

McNally smiled.

The Indian moved closer to the campfire. He shivered and coughed several times before finally lying down on one side.

"He's sleeping," said Calhoun.

After waiting several minutes to make certain the Indian was asleep, Calhoun and McNally stood up. Calhoun directed McNally to slip around in a half circle and get to about fifteen feet from the campfire and the Indian.

When Calhoun was sure his partner was in position, he himself crept forward from the thorn bush. He heard the Indian snoring as he moved closer. The campfire was burning low, but still crackling, drowning out the sound of the Ranger's footsteps.

Calhoun slipped to within a few feet. The Indian rolled over slightly, but showed no sign of waking.

Calhoun gripped his knife, crouched low and tiptoed to within arm's length.

An owl hooted in the distance and the Indian rolled over, then coughed again, this time violently. He was shivering and perspiring at the same time; probably ill and feverish, maybe delirious.

Calhoun was now only inches away. He thrust his

knife toward the sleeping Indian's chest—just as the man's eyes opened and locked onto Calhoun's face. The Indian quickly rolled to one side, just in time to avoid the knife.

Calhoun lost his balance and pitched forward, dropping the knife as he hit the hard ground. He rolled over to see the Indian standing over him, large and stocky, clutching the Bowie knife.

Panic gripped Calhoun and he felt a burst of dampness spreading over his crotch. The Indian lunged forward.

"No . . . please . . . no," Calhoun whispered.

The Indian suddenly staggered, let the knife fall, and stumbled forward. He dropped to the ground beside Calhoun. Calhoun jerked upright to see a bloodstain spreading across the Indian's lower back.

McNally stood several feet away, holding a bloodstained spear. His face showed ashen in the fading light of the campfire.

Calhoun rose slowly to his feet. The Indian was obviously dead. To make certain, however, Calhoun snatched up the Bowie knife and ran the blade across the man's throat. Blood spurted into the brown dirt, staining Calhoun's boots.

Calhoun wiped perspiration from his face. "What took you so long?" he spat at McNally.

"I had to move slowly. It was dark."

"Where'd you get the spear?"

"Found it over there with his supplies." McNally pointed to several blankets and large leather sacks on the ground nearby. "Let's see what else he has." McNally walked over to the sacks and opened them, then grinned. "Well, lookee here."

"What'd you find?"

"Chewin' tobaccer. This is our lucky day. Also seems to be some jerky and nuts in here."

McNally and Calhoun hoisted the leather sacks to their shoulders and started back to their horses. Suddenly McNally stopped and pointed to markings in the dirt, faintly visible in the flickering light of the campfire. "Look."

Calhoun shrugged. "So?

"The Injun wasn't alone."

"He's alone now."

"One man couldn't have made all those marks alone. He has companions."

"Well, where are they? I don't see 'em."

"They're out there somewhere." McNally frowned. "Must be out hunting. They left this one behind. He didn't look so good . . . maybe he was sick."

"Well, we'd best be going, right?"

"You know, the captain ain't gonna like this."

"We ain't telling him anything."

"He'll ask about these bags and the tobaccer."

"We found 'em out here. They were just here . . . maybe fell off a cart?"

"He ain't gonna believe that."

"What the good captain believes ain't no concern of mine," Calhoun snapped.

They mounted their horses and left the dead Indian

lying in the dirt beside the smoldering campfire. As they rode into the darkness, Calhoun cursed silently at the sensation of his urine-soaked pants pressing against his skin.

CHAPTER XII

Felipe Baca had never been quite the same after the blow on the head he had received from the American soldier. He had lain unconscious for a day and ill for several weeks longer; Petra, Antonio, and María tended to him day and night. Felipe finally recovered his physical health, but a silent fire of hatred burned within him.

It was a hatred shared by most of the locals, and with good reason. Changes came rapidly to *el Reyno de Nuevo México* after the American conquest. None other than Charles Bent was appointed territorial governor by General Stephen Watts Kearny. Kearny soon left New Mexico, leading his conquering troops on to California; Kit Carson accompanied him. There, Kearny's forces were nearly defeated by fierce Mexican resistance, but eventually California fell to the American army.

Back in New Mexico, americano soldiers were now seen constantly on the streets of Taos and at Aguírre's trading post. They were an unruly and bullying lot, demanding food, lodging, and even women. They spoke with arrogant contempt of the "greasers", as they called New Mexicans.

"A month ago these gringos were shoveling mierda in Missouri," Jesús Aguírre whispered to Antonio one afternoon, as they stood in front of the trading post. It was now mid-September and, although the air was still warm, a hint of autumn hung in the air. A large álamo on the Taos plaza nearby was already showing signs of yellow and gold in its leaves.

A group of soldiers sauntered past the trading post. "Look at them now, these Missouri volunteers, strutting about Taos acting like gods," Jesús muttered. The blue-coated soldiers glared at Jesús and Antonio but continued past the trading post without slowing down, heading on down the dirt path encircling the plaza. Jesús and Antonio watched them pass the flagpole that now flew the American flag.

"The people call them *goddammees*," Jesús told Antonio.

"Why is that?"

"Because that is the word they speak so often . . . *god damn*."

"Are they here to stay?" asked Antonio.

"I'm afraid so," said Jesús.

"How will we manage?"

"I don't know. Somehow, we will survive all of this."

"México did not fight hard enough to hold our land," Antonio said sadly. Jesús nodded. "The mexicanos are weak and divided. The americanos knew this and took advantage of our weakness."

"Such a loss," said Antonio. "And such a tragedy."

"And we endured their coarse manners so long because they were guests in our land." Jesús crossed his hands across his chest. "It is not just we, que somos mexicanos, who are angry. The puebleños hate the americanos too. The soldiers have taken the Indians' grain and attacked their women. American missionaries and preachers have also removed the crucifixes from our churches. And they are demanding that we speak only their language inside my store." Jesús shook his head in disgust. "Can you believe such arrogance?"

"I've heard talk of resistance," Antonio said. "Nothing in particular, just talk of fighting."

"I have heard the same thing."

"But how could we succeed? We have few weapons. We would need an army to overcome the americanos."

"It does seem futile," said Jesús. "A rebellion would only result in death and destruction."

"So we must endure the arrogance and insults of los americanos?"

"I do not like these gringos any more than you do, Antonio. We are being treated as foreigners in our own land. But what can we do? I have a store to run . . . I have a family to feed. I have no choice but to cater to these people."

"What about Felipe?"

Jesús shrugged his shoulders sadly. "I know, Antonio. Believe me, *I know.* I can't say for certain what we should do. All I know is that in these times we have to look after our families. That is the most we can do. You have a wife now. Take care of my daughter. Look after her."

Antonio had recognized the truth in his father-in-law's words. "I will, Jesús, I will."

Evening had fallen over the llano by the time Antonio rode up the sharp incline of rock and cactus. The faint outline of a trail led to the top of a broad, flat mesa that he remembered as Mesa Rica from his Cibolero days. The trail had been forged over hundreds of years by buffalo that made their way up to feed on the rich grasses atop the mesa. From here, Antonio would have an open view of the llano once the sun rose. He and his uncle had often climbed this mesa to spy on the vast buffalo herds that once roamed the valleys to the east. Those herds had largely vanished now.

Antonio had lost the horse tracks several miles below the mesa, but he expected to find the trail again on the opposite side. The top of the mesa was long and flat and seemed to extend into a limitless expanse in the moonlight. Deciding to camp for the night, Antonio dismounted and led his horse, looking for a likely spot.

As he trudged through the chilly darkness, a figure emerged from the shadows and the barrel of a rifle glinted in the dusk. Antonio suddenly found himself facing a young boy, perhaps only ten years old, holding a rifle.

Mexican or Indian? Antonio was unable to see the

boy's face clearly. "Habla español, muchacho?" he asked.

The boy answered, "Sí."

Antonio raised his arms slightly. "I mean you no harm."

The boy moved closer. "Go away. This is *my* pasture."

"I'm only passing through."

The boy was silent.

"You're a brave one," Antonio said. "Why are you alone here on the mesa?"

"I take care of the sheep."

Antonio looked up and for a moment thought he saw the ground move in the darkness. Then he realized that an immense number of sheep were grazing in the pastures ahead. *There must be several thousand sheep out there.* "What is your name?" he asked.

"Diego."

"Mucho gusto, Diego. I am Antonio."

"Why are you here?"

"I'm looking for someone," said Antonio.

Diego smiled. "En la Mesa Rica? There is no one here but me and the sheep."

"May I stay here for the night? I'll be moving on in the morning."

The boy lowered his rifle and gestured toward the flocks of sheep. "I have a camp nearby."

Antonio could see the boy's haggard face clearly now. Diego was obviously tired and hungry.

Antonio followed Diego past the grazing sheep and

to a makeshift camp consisting of a bedroll and a dead campfire. "You are here alone?"

"Yes," Diego said.

"And your family?"

"In La Cuesta."

"You're a long way from home."

The boy put on a brave face, but Antonio saw sadness in his eyes. "How long have you been here?" asked Antonio.

"Six weeks," said Diego. "Mi padre es un partidero. He herds sheep for the rich gringo companies out of Las Vegas and Santa Fe."

Antonio was well aware of the semifeudal *partido* system that had originated in New Mexico and had later been picked up and exploited by the Americans. Diego's father must be a sharecropper, herding sheep owned by the gringo landowners in return for a tiny percentage of the herd—minus any losses to the herd as a whole. Most partideros were hopelessly in debt to their employers and lived in virtual slavery.

Antonio was amazed that the partideros had ventured this far into the llano, where attacks from Indians and marauding Texas gringos were a constant risk. *Diego's father must be desperate for livelihood, to have left the boy here alone to tend the sheep,* thought Antonio. He asked, "When will your father return for you?"

"I hope to see him in a few weeks," the boy said sadly.

"You miss your home and family?"

"Yes," Diego said. Antonio thought he saw tears in the boy's eyes.

"How old are you, son?"

"Eleven years."

A year older than Antonio had guessed. In some ways, however, the boy seemed even older. Fear and loneliness had evidently aged him.

"Let me help you start a campfire," said Antonio.

"No!"

"Why not?"

The boy hesitated. "Well . . . two days ago I was tending sheep at the far rim of the mesa and I heard noises from the valley. Then I saw a group of Indians passing below on horseback. I counted five of them. They stopped to camp for the night. They did not see me, and I kept my campfire cold that night because I was afraid."

"Are they still down there?"

"No. The Indians left yesterday. But one of their party remained behind, while the others were hunting. I saw all of this from here on the mesa."

"If they are gone now, why are you fearful?"

The boy explained: "That night I climbed down the mesa for a closer look. I saw two gringos ride into the Indian camp. They killed the man who stayed behind. The other four Indians returned that evening. I thought they might come looking for those who had murdered their companion and that they might find and blame me, so I spent the night in the cold again. The Indians were gone this morning."

"You have courage," Antonio said, handing the boy some carne seca. A cool breeze blew through the camp and the boy shivered.

"It's cold here," Antonio told Diego. "You need to make yourself a fire."

"I'm afraid," the boy admitted.

"Surely there's nothing to fear now," Antonio said reassuringly. "You've been here for six weeks already. You'll get through this."

"But the gringos who killed the Indian . . ."

"Do not worry, my young friend."

"But will they come back and try to kill me?"

Antonio smiled slightly, touched by the boy's fear. "They would have already been here. You're safe now. They must be gone."

An expression of relief spread gradually across the boy's face.

Antonio continued: "The gringo horsemen are gone from this area, and I am sure those Indians will not return either. We're not in any danger. Let's get a fire going." He proceeded to help the boy prepare a camp- fire and bed down for the night.

Diego was already tending to the sheep when Antonio awoke the next morning. As Antonio got to his feet, he saw Diego pause to examine the lance hanging from the horse's saddle. "You are a hunter?" asked Diego.

"I was a hunter . . . un Cibolero."

"I've heard stories of the Ciboleros from my grand- father. Are you hunting buffalo?"

"No, not buffalo, but I *am* hunting."

"I wish I could go with you," Diego said. "I wish I could leave this place."

"You're better off here, Diego. Your father will return for you soon."

"I don't want you to leave."

"You'll be fine here, Diego. Be brave and be strong." Antonio mounted his horse and rode off. He glanced back for a last look at the flocks of sheep, meandering atop the mesa like so many specks of white against a sea of green. The mesa was lush from the rains of the llano; Mesa Rica was well named. Before the sheep herders came, great numbers of buffalo had roamed these heights.

At the rim of the mesa, Antonio dismounted to survey the jagged green valleys far below. Looking down from this height was like standing atop a mountain. In a sense, Mesa Rica *was* a mountain, with its dizzying and sometimes foreboding heights. In the morning sunlight, a great escarpment of rock and cliffs could be seen skirting the eastern horizon like a fortress wall protecting the plains beyond. The landscape below Mesa Rica seemed particularly difficult, dotted with precipitous rises and falls and abundant yucca and piñon. *Tough to navigate,* he thought. *But not impossible.* A *gallineta,* a small roadrunner, darted past him and down the cliffs.

Below, Antonio could see the ashes of the campfire Diego had mentioned. He rode down to examine the area. There were numerous tracks of unshod horses— probably the Indians'—and two sets of horseshoe tracks leading off in another direction. Antonio recognized those tracks. The two riders had apparently broken off from the group, and now were likely heading back to the remaining Rangers.

They continue to ride to the southeast, Antonio thought. After murdering the black man, the Tejanos had come this way, bypassing Mesa Rica and killing the Indian in the process.

Antonio gazed intently at the valleys spreading eastward toward the lands of the Tejanos. *Lands that once belonged to Nuevo México,* he thought, feeling fresh apprehension for his daughter's situation. *I'm getting closer to her. I know it. I can feel it. The Tejanos do not know these lands like I do. If she can only hold on . . . if Elena can only survive.*

Thirty miles east of Mesa Rica near a small ravine, Captain Travis Russell heaved a sigh of frustration and paced angrily beside his horse.

"It was just some Injun," Calhoun said. "I don't understand what the fuss is all about."

Despite Calhoun's warning not to tell the captain what had happened, McNally had soon been bragging about killing the Indian and stealing his tobacco and supplies. Now Captain Russell was furious.

"This is not the first time you've disobeyed my orders," he barked at Calhoun. *And not the last,* he could almost hear Calhoun thinking.

"Do you have any idea what you've done?" Russell demanded.

The two men were silent for a moment, and then McNally said with obvious pride, "We killed ourselves an Injun."

"This is Comanche country," Russell reminded them.

Calhoun smirked. "Well, now there's one less to worry about."

"Where there's one Comanche," Russell growled, "there are others. Do you *understand* what I'm trying to tell you?" Russell paced furiously. "I've taken enough from you. When we get back to Waco, I'm bringing both of you up for dereliction of duty."

"My pa won't be happy about this," said Calhoun.

Russell shouted, "Enough!"

McNally moaned, "But, Captain—"

Russell cut him short. "There's nothing else to be said. At this point, it's only a question of the extent of the charges against you. Now get ready to ride. We're moving out."

Calhoun breathed a sigh of frustration and stalked away. McNally stumbled after him as Russell leaned against his horse, his head swimming with frustration. He glanced at their captive, seated on the hard ground nearby with her wrists bound.

The other Rangers packed their few belongings and prepared their horses for the ride ahead. Russell signaled the girl to mount. He caught a glimpse of the fear in her eyes and nodded sympathetically, careful not to let the others see.

A sense of foreboding hovered over Russell. He doubted the murdered Indian had been traveling alone.

Chapter XIII

On an early October day years earlier, a snowstorm had settled over Taos Valley, blanketing the village and Indian Pueblo in a layer of delicate white. Heavy dark clouds had hovered over the Sangre de Cristo Mountains while Felipe Baca and his wife rested in their small home near her father's trading post. The one-room house, a simple and inviting adobe structure, had been built to keep Felipe and Petra warm during the coming winter.

Felipe pushed open the bars of a shutter and stared into the dark night. Everything was quiet. A bright moon cast a pale glow over Taos. He shivered and stepped back, letting the shutters fall closed.

"It's a cold night," he told Petra. "I expect it will be a bitter winter. The snows are earlier than last year."

Petra sat on a chair stitching a large cloth in her lap. A small fire crackled in the adobe hearth in the corner, casting an orange glow throughout the room. "You are always busy, my love," she said.

Enchanted by her loveliness, he could not help but smile. She smiled back, the reflection from the fireplace making her flushing cheeks even rosier.

In recent weeks, Felipe had thrown himself into his job at the trading post, spending long days tending to patrons and stocking supplies. While he worked at the post with Antonio and their father-in-law, Petra had turned to sewing for additional income.

Soon she will have other work to do, Felipe thought. Petra would give birth to their first child in eight months. The thought of having a family pleased Felipe. He looked forward to the new life that awaited both of them.

"I will only sew for another hour, and then we will go to sleep," she said.

"Very well. But I need to rest. Tomorrow promises to be another long day at your father's trading post."

"It will be your business someday," she said. "My father has grown to see you and your brother Antonio as his sons."

"Your father is a good man," he said, and then abruptly paused as he felt a sharp pain in his temple. He staggered to the narrow bed on the opposite side of the room.

Petra stopped working and looked at him anxiously. "The pain in your head again?"

"Yes." Felipe rubbed his forehead with the palms of his hands and lay down on the bed. The pain was unbearable, like a sharp rock pounding the inside of his skull. Though he had recovered from the physical marks of the americano soldier's blow, he still suffered periodic headaches. Lately, the pain was becoming increasingly severe.

"Las yerbas?" Petra asked. "Do you have any left?"

"No," he gasped.

"I'll get some more from la curandera." Petra slid her needle into the fabric and stood up, placing the sewing on a nearby chest.

"No," insisted Felipe. "It is too late. I'll be fine." He closed his eyes tightly and grimaced against the pain.

"Nonsense!" Petra said firmly, wrapping herself in a heavy shawl. "She doesn't live that far from here."

She wasn't even certain Felipe saw her leave. He was sprawled on the bed, groaning in agony.

Petra stepped into the frigid night air. The streets of Taos were hushed. She hurried toward the plaza, snow crunching beneath her feet. Soon, she reached the small hut on the opposite side of the plaza where lived the old woman who provided pain-soothing herbs.

The frail curandera with stringy white hair and missing front teeth answered Petra's knock. "Ah, you are the wife of Felipe, the brave one who was injured by the americano soldiers."

Petra nodded. "Yes."

A gust of cold wind enveloped both women. The old woman shivered. "Mi hijita, come inside where it's warm. You'll catch a cold out there."

Petra followed the old woman inside.

"You are such a lovely girl." The woman motioned toward a bentwood rocker.

"Thank you," said Petra, sitting down and pulling her rebozo closer around her shoulders.

The old woman lived by herself and was rumored to have been a beauty in her youth. Her husband had died many years earlier. He had been *muy rico in la cap-ital—Ciudad de México*—and had settled in New Mexico at the end of the last century. He had made a fortune on the caravan routes north from Nueva España into Nuevo México, but had died penniless, having lost his wealth in the gambling dens of Santa Fe and Taos. Within a few years, his widow had established herself as a compassionate and knowledgeable curandera, prescribing herbal cures for many of her neighbors. The New Mexicans revered las curanderas. They were the lifeblood of the isolated village communities, offering herbs and prayers during times of sickness and grief.

"I have something here that will help you." The old woman reached into a ceramic jar decorated with a Pueblo Indian motif. She removed a handful of dried dark green leaves, crumbled them into a pouch, and tied it shut with a small piece of string.

"Oshá?" Petra asked.

The old woman shook her head. "No, este es mejor, alta misa de la sierra." This was a rare and highly valued medicinal herb that grew in the forests of the Sangre de Cristo Mountains.

"Muchas gracias," Petra responded with relief. She handed the old woman several pesos. "I hope this is enough. If not, I can knit you a blanket, or sew you clothing if you would like."

"That is perfectly fine, mi hijita." The woman gave Petra the pouch with the herbs. "Prepare this as a tea for your husband. Use it sparingly. I will have to wait until the summer before I can climb the mountain again."

"I cannot tell you how thankful I am."

The old woman was pleased. "Stay for a while, mi hijita. I was cooking some posole. You can have some."

"I would love to, but Felipe is ill. I must get back to him as soon as possible."

"Yes, that is best. Go to your husband. These herbs will help him."

"Thank you."

Petra stepped out into the crisp cold night and glanced up at the moon. The surrounding Sangre de Cristo Mountains were faintly visible in its light. She hurried back across the snow-covered plaza and past her father's trading post. Soon she saw her jacal in the distance.

Suddenly, three figures materialized out of the night. At first glance, Petra thought they were simply passersby, local people like herself. But as they grew closer and became clearly discernible, fear gripped her. The men were blue-coated soldiers with yellow stripes on their shoulders—and they were clearly inebriated.

They stepped in front of her and one spoke. "Lookee what we got here!"

Another solider added, "A beautiful little señorita, just what we was looking for.

Petra's heart pounded. She ducked her head and attempted to move away from the americano soldiers without making a sound.

The tallest man blocked her path. "Where are you going, little lady? Don't you want to have yourself a fine American man? We're much better than those lazy greasers."

Laughter filled the air. Petra felt hands grabbing at her. She yanked away and broke into a run.

She only got a few yards before one of the soldiers caught up. He spun her around and pulled her to him. His hand covered her mouth, choking off her scream. She fought back, throwing her arms into the air, struggling to hit and claw her way from the other men gathered around.

Her surging terror quickly gave way to a black nothingness.

Antonio pushed aside the painful memories and peered through the old American cavalry field glasses he had picked up years before in Santa Fe. The scenery shimmered in the afternoon heat. Some distance away, he could see four Indians—perhaps Comanches—riding over the high sandstone bluffs. The afternoon heat blazed across a landscape of green grasses and brown cliffs. They were headed southeast, as if they also were following the path of the Tejanos. Perhaps these were the men whose companion had been killed; even from this distance, Antonio could sense a certain anger and determination in their movements.

He followed them, careful to remain out of sight. Like the llaneros and other Indians of the plains, Antonio had long ago developed an intuitive talent for locating his position from the shape of the land, the bushes and trees, and even the color of the sky. Right now, the clear turquoise sky seemed to surround and overwhelm the ground. The ambience was very different from the high desert and mountains further west in el Reyno; the overall effect here was almost oppressive.

In this portion of the llano, water was scarce. Antonio knew, however, that numerous *playas* could be found in the llano. At such small basins, replenished by the rains of the llano, the Ciboleros had rested and watered their horses during long autumn hunts. But the basins were extremely difficult to see until someone was almost on top of them. Antonio had heard of men dying of thirst only a few yards from playas overflowing with water.

To the Tejanos the liana is a useless desert, Antonio thought. *To the Indians and Ciboleros, it is a world filled with life.* He spurred his horse forward as the Indians disappeared beyond the bluffs. *Lead me to the Tejanos, my friends, lead me to them. . . .*

Petra's body had been found in the early morning snow. It fell to Antonio to break the news to Felipe. On reaching his brother's home, Antonio had found Felipe on the floor, unconscious from the previous night's seizure. Several hours passed before Felipe finally awakened. He immediately asked about Petra.

As delicately as he could, Antonio explained what had happened. He saw Felipe's face contort into mixed grief, disbelief, and rage. Felipe sprang to his feet and raced out the front door of the jacal. His scream echoed through the streets: "No!"

Antonio went outside to find his brother kneeling in the snow, sobbing. "I am sorry, Felipe."

"Where is her body?"

"In the back room at the trading post. Jesús is there now."

Felipe staggered to his feet with dazed eyes. He staggered and Antonio caught his arm.

"I don't understand," Felipe whispered as they made their way from the jacal to the trading post.

A crowd of familiar faces had gathered inside; the word had already spread through Taos. Antonio led Felipe to the back room where Jesús, his wife, and other family members were assembled. Every head hung low. Several old women wailed in grief.

Petra's body lay on a table with a thin cloth covering her face. Antonio stared at the young woman, so full of life and promise only a day earlier. *Where is God when we need Him?*

María stood near her sister's body. Antonio embraced his weeping wife as Felipe stumbled toward Petra and gently removed the cloth. Her delicate face was bruised and battered. Felipe collapsed with a sob.

Jesús and Antonio helped Felipe into a wooden chair in one corner. Felipe sat motionless, staring with a blank expression, as if his mind were entirely gone.

It was too much for Antonio to bear. He turned away

and stumbled into the room where the larger crowd had gathered. Voices murmured around him as he pushed toward the door.

"Pobre Petra. No woman deserves this fate," someone said.

Another whispered, "Gringo soldiers were seen in the area last night near where Petra was found."

Antonio staggered out into the frigid Taos air. The sky was bright blue and the sun cast its rays across the snow-covered landscape, but Antonio saw no beauty in the day. His heart ached for his brother and *cuñada*. And poor María—she had doted on her younger sister. The two were so much alike.

Antonio made his way to a pale brown adobe structure located off the plaza. This had until recently been the offices of the Alcalde of Taos. The recently appointed Sheriff of Taos now occupied the building, which also served as a jail. The name "Sheriff" itself was foreign and strange to Antonio and the New Mexicans, but Antonio understood the Sheriff to be a lawman of some sort.

Antonio entered the building to find a muscular, sandy-haired man seated behind an old wooden desk. A tall, thin man with a beard stood nearby, silently reading a document. Three blue-uniformed soldiers stood opposite the desk. The soldiers appeared haggard and tired. They reeked of alcohol and their faces were uneasy.

Antonio heard the man behind the desk speak in a low voice to the soldiers. "You'd best be getting out of

Taos now. Go to Santa Fe. Governor Bent will see to your safety."

The three men walked out past Antonio. He waited silently by the desk.

The man at the desk looked at Antonio. "What can I do for you?"

Antonio recognized this man as Stephen Louis Lee, a frequent customer at the trading post. Lee had immigrated to Taos years earlier, converted to Catholicism from his original Presbyterianism, and become a naturalized Mexican citizen. He had subsequently married a Taos Mexican woman and started a distilling business, eventually becoming an important and influential presence in the American community of Taos. Lee had also received co-ownership of a million-acre grant on the west side of the Sangre de Cristo mountain range. Unlike many influential and wealthy Americans, Lee was generally considered a sincere and fair man.

"You're the sheriff?" Antonio asked.

"Recently appointed," Lee responded, and then gestured at the older bearded man. "This is James Armstrong."

"I'm an attorney." Armstrong smiled and extended his hand in greeting. Antonio shook it, but his heart wasn't in the welcome. He had heard Armstrong's name before, in association with an americano who was filing claims in Santa Fe to steal Spanish and Mexican land grants.

"You're Antonio Baca, right?" the sheriff asked.

Antonio nodded. He looked at both men and spoke

slowly in English. "My brother's wife, Petra Baca Aguírre, has been murdered."

The sheriff reclined awkwardly in his chair. He seemed uncomfortable. "Right . . . Yes. I heard that a woman was found dead this morning."

"Quite a tragedy," Armstrong said. Somehow, Antonio did not sense any genuine compassion in the attorney's voice.

Lee seemed more sympathetic. He nodded his head slowly. "I knew Petra. I also know your father-in-law. He's a good man."

"Petra was brutalized by these animals, these soldiers," Antonio said.

"Your sister-in-law's death is a great tragedy." The sheriff glanced at a jail cell at the rear of the room. Two men, who appeared to be Indians, sat on the floor inside. "Believe me, I want to help you, Mr. Baca, but I have to handle these men first. We're having problems again at the pueblo. I'll have to look into your complaint later."

Antonio raised an eyebrow. "A *complaint?*"

"We're occupied with other matters now."

Antonio was indignant. "A woman is dead, and her death amounts to merely a *complaint?* How can anything be more important?"

"I'm the sheriff; I have to keep order and peace in *all* matters."

"And *justice?*"

"Of course," Lee said. "We Americans came to your land to bring you justice and democracy and . . . to . . .

uh . . . liberate you from Mexican tyranny."

"Pero somos mexicanos," Antonio said forcefully.

"Speak English," Armstrong said irritably. "This is the United States of America. We speak English. Com-pren-day?"

"I am *not* an American, Mr. Armstrong. My family, the people of this village, and my countrymen have always been Mexican citizens. This is our home; this is our land."

Armstrong rolled his eyes dismissively.

Antonio turned away from Armstrong and looked directly at the Sherriff. "You've lived in el Reyno for many years. Surely *you* speak the language of los españoles."

"I do," Lee said. "My wife is Mexican, just like you. She was born here in Taos. This is her home too. I know how you feel, Mr. Baca."

"This is American territory now," Armstrong interrupted. "We speak only English here."

Lee looked unhappily at the attorney. "That's quite enough, Mr. Armstrong."

Antonio struggled to remain calm. "There are witnesses who saw soldiers in the area where my sister-in-law was murdered."

"Did these people see the murder itself?" asked Lee.

"I don't know."

"Can they identify the men in question?"

"I'm not certain."

"Well," said Lee, "I promise I will try to talk to them later."

Antonio was dumbfounded. "You call yourself a lawman? You should take immediate action. Go to Aguírre's trading post. There are men there now you should talk with."

"I promise I will—soon, Mr. Baca."

Antonio leaned forward and slammed his fist on the desk. "No más tarde! Ahora!" He felt his heart beating faster as disbelief combined with rage surged through his body.

Lee stood up and put a hand on Antonio's shoulder. The sheriff's eyes were sad and helpless. "Please, go home."

Antonio turned and stomped out the door. *This sheriff is useless.* Lee obviously had little experience as a lawman and even less authority to act against American interests by bringing Petra's killers to justice. Between Armstrong's antipathy and Sheriff Lee's haplessness, Antonio knew there was no help to be found here.

CHAPTER XIV

Russell maneuvered his horse to the edge of the precipice and stared down into a narrow gorge between the sharply rising canyon walls. Smith, the preacher, brought his horse to a halt alongside. The other Rangers paused several yards away to rest. Several dismounted, along with the Mexican girl, who stood passively to one side. She looked worn out and exhausted.

Russell wiped the perspiration from his forehead and smacked his lips. He was thirsty. "We're low on water," he said softly.

"We've been low for days," Smith complained. "But we're getting close. Look down there."

Russell saw the outline of a meandering river far below.

"Sure looks good," Smith said with a smile. "A gift from the Almighty."

Russell shook his head slowly. "Maybe not."

"Why do you say that?"

"Look for yourself." Russell pointed at the steep canyon walls below. "We can't climb down that way. It's too risky. And we could lose a day or more trying to find another way into the canyon."

"We might die of thirst in this wasteland if we don't try." Smith shook his head. "This country is strange. The land's been flat for miles; now suddenly it changes. Where on earth did this canyon come from?"

"I don't know. But the river seems to cut this way from the northwest."

"We're going to need water soon."

"Maybe you can do a little praying for us, preacher. You always act like you have a direct contact with Jesus himself," Russell said sarcastically.

Smith bristled visibly. "Well, where are we, anyway?"

"That might be the Canadian River down there, but I don't know. We entered New Mexico territory from the north. The rest of this country has yet to be explored and charted."

"But we're still heading southeast, right?"

"Yes," said Russell. "As far as I can tell." He licked his dry lips and scanned the desolate countryside. "The truth is, I think we're being followed."

Smith shrugged that off and persisted, "But we *are* in Texas?"

"I'm guessing we are, maybe a day across the border. But in this wasteland, we might as well be in a foreign country."

"And what about water?"

"I think we'd better keep moving. With luck, we'll soon find some within easy reach."

Petra had been buried in a small cemetery at the edge of Taos. For over two hundred years, this burial ground beneath the majestic snow-covered mountains had received the local people.

Antonio had stood in the cold Taos air that day, saying a silent good-bye to his sister-in-law. María leaned on his arm. A large crowd of Taoseños had gathered to support the family.

Petra's wooden coffin was lowered into a rectangular-shaped hole. The surrounding mountains rose majestically over the cemetery. The family wept softly, their tears dropping to form tiny crystals in the alabaster snow.

As the crowd began to dissipate, Antonio accompanied María back to the trading post. He left her there with her father and Felipe, and walked out into the muddy streets of Taos, trying to clear his mind.

As he neared an open field, he heard shouts and drumbeats. A group of men were gathered in the field, surrounded by a crowd of bystanders and clad in what appeared to be armor. Some men were dressed in ancient military regalia with metal breastplates. Others held bows and arrows, or old-style Spanish colonial muskets. Some were clad in Comanche garments. A great cry went up from the bystanders as several of the armored men charged each other against the backdrop of the Sangre de Cristo Mountains.

"Los Comanches," came a familiar voice at Antonio's elbow.

Antonio turned and saw Jesús standing beside him. "I'm surprised you are here."

"I need to be outside. Too much sorrow back at the trading post. I followed you here."

"But the family?"

"They will understand," said Jesús. "My daughter will understand."

"Yes, María is patient."

"No, I meant Petra. She would understand on a day such as this." Jesús pointed to the crowd gathered in the field before them. "The drama being performed is known as Los Comanches. It is the story of Cuerno Verde, the great Comanche Indian Chief."

Antonio nodded and glanced back at the armored men. "I have heard of Los Comanches, but have never seen it myself. It celebrates the defeat of Cuerno Verde."

"Yes, many of the northern villages perform this

play. It reminds us of the sacrifices and suffering of our forefathers. Perhaps this is a fitting day for my daughter to be buried, the day we celebrate the drama of Los Comanches. You see that actor there?" Jesús pointed at a man with a staff in one hand and a spear in the other. "He is playing the role of Cuerno Verde."

Antonio vaguely recalled the story of Cuerno Verde—Green Horn—and his defeat at the hands of Governor De Anza's soldiers. The great Comanche chief had been killed in battle in 1778, near the mountain New Mexicans called *El Capitán.*

"Those were different times, before the coming of the americanos," Antonio said.

"Maybe not so different," said Jesús. "This drama is said to have been written by a soldier from Taos who served with De Anza. The governor had been sent by the viceroy to el Reyno to deal with Indian raids. For many years, the Comanches had attacked our northern villages, killing not only our people but also the Pueblo Indians. De Anza finally organized an expedition north in the winter of 1778 to deal with the Comanche threat once and for all. The puebleños and the Spanish joined forces to march north against the Comanches."

Los Comanches continued to play out while Jesús narrated the history: "As you can see, Cuerno Verde was a great warrior, well respected by the Spanish. But his death and the defeat of his army ended the Comanche attacks on Taos."

Jesús suddenly became quietly pensive.

"You know, Antonio, our people are again ready to fight. There is talk of rebellion to expel the foreigners from our land."

"It would be a dangerous undertaking."

"Of course," Jesús admitted.

"Do you intend to join the resistance? What of your business, and your family?"

Jesús paused and then asked, "And what of the harm these animals have done to my family?"

Antonio said cautiously, "But the americanos have superior weapons."

"This is our homeland, Antonio. We must defend it to prevent any more brutality."

"I understand," said Antonio. "But what of unity? Without it, rebellion is hopeless. The americanos marched into our land without any resistance on our part. Our own people are still divided. And would the puebleños work with us?"

"Yes, they are ready to join us. This is their land too, and the americanos despise los indios almost as much as they do our people."

Antonio was intrigued, yet plagued with misgivings. Images flooded his mind: americanos swaggering arrogantly through the streets of Taos, Felipe crumbling under a blow from a soldier's rifle, Petra lying in a grave.

"I've been asked to meet with some interested parties." Jesús looked meaningfully into Antonio's eyes. "Would you like to join me?"

Antonio took a deep breath. "Yes."

It was a short walk to the great Taos Pueblo, the home of the Taos Indians who had occupied the area for over a thousand years. After years of Spanish colonial occupation and Indian revolt, the Taos Indians had finally settled down to live in peace near the villagers of Taos. But the peace was uneasy. Memories of the great Pueblo revolt of 1680, which had expelled the Spanish from New Mexico for ten years, still lived on both sides after more than a century and a half.

As they walked together, Jesús reminisced aloud about the days after the revolt, after the Spaniards had returned to reoccupy the land by force. "My grandfather told us of those times. Following the reconquista of New Mexico, the Spanish agreed to let the Indians maintain their traditional religion and way of life, paying only nominal homage to the Catholic Church. The Indians in turn came to rely on the Spanish for protection from the nomadic Jicarilla Apaches to the west and the great Comanche tribes from the north and east. Spanish and Mexican authorities helped the Pueblo Indians to arm for defense against the Apaches and Comanches."

Glittering in the winter sun, the great adobe structures of the Taos Pueblo seemed to rise endlessly into the sky. *The pueblo is so close . . . and yet so far.*

An Indian greeted Jesús as they entered the Taos Pueblo. Antonio recalled seeing this man at the trading post, but did not remember his name.

"Thank you for coming," the Indian said, wrapping his arms around Jesús in *un abrazo.*

"My heart is heavy on this day," said Jesús with a sad smile.

"My family is very sorry for your loss," the Indian said.

"This is Antonio, husband of my daughter María."

"Mucho gusto," said Antonio, shaking the Indian's hand.

"Mucho gusto," the man replied. "My name is Tomasito. Bienvenidos."

Antonio and Jesús followed Tomasito into a small one-room adobe house among an interconnected mass of similar structures, built on top of each other like a series of steps. Two other men were seated at a table in the center of the room. One was dark and short, perhaps in his mid-thirties; the other, fair skinned with blue eyes and a white beard, seemed much older.

Tomasito closed the door and brought out coffee and bread.

"Thank you for your hospitality," said Jesús. He and Tomasito sat down at the table, but Antonio remained standing.

"Antonio," said Tomasito, nodding to the oldest man, "this is Pablo Herrera." Herrera shook Antonio's hand. "Yes, you are el Cibolero? Jesús has spoken very highly of you."

"Mucho gusto," Antonio responded.

"And this is Mañuel Cortez," Tomasito said, gesturing to the remaining man. Antonio now recalled that both men were leading citizens of Taos.

Tomasito continued, "What we talk of now, we must keep in secrecy."

Jesús nodded. "Of course."

"We all know why we are here. I hardly need elaborate on the injustices my people have suffered in recent months," said Tomasito. "The soldiers have taken our cattle and stores of maíze, and have bullied and insulted us. Our women have been attacked by soldiers, and some of our men beaten and killed." He looked sympathetically at Jesús. "And your people have suffered as much from the invaders' arrogance and violence. Whatever differences we have had between us in the past must now be set aside."

"The village of Taos is ready to fight," said Herrera. "And I've been in touch with community leaders from Santa Cruz down to Bernalillo, Atrisco, and Alburquerque. They are all willing to join us."

The mention of Atrisco reminded Antonio of his family still living there. He had not seen his mother or father in over a year; he wondered how they were faring under the occupation.

"I think we can count on most of the northern Pueblos," said Tomasito, "and perhaps some of the Jicarilla Apache bands to the west."

"What of Mora and Las Vegas and the villages to the east of the Sangre de Cristo?" asked Mañuel Cortez.

"They're too firmly under the grip of the americano soldiers. A fort is already being constructed to the east. I don't think we can expect any help from Las Vegas."

Herrera poured himself another cup of coffee. "And México?"

"The government is fully occupied with the Amer-

162

ican army's push toward el capital," Jesús said.

"Pobres," said Cortez.

"Perhaps we could rely on some troops from the northern provinces of México," Jesús said, "maybe Chihuahua, but it's doubtful."

"These americanos and their *manifest destiny,*" Herrera growled.

The others looked at him in puzzlement.

"It's the American philosophy," Herrera explained. "I heard it from one of their merchants in Santa Fe several weeks ago. They believe that God has anointed them to seize the lands of the Americas and spread their language and culture even to those who have no desire for these things. Any culture or people not of their own thinking is considered worthless and in need of civilizing. The americanos call this their 'manifest destiny.' "

Jesús set his jaw with determination. "There are still many more of us than of them here in el Reyno. And despite the soldiers they've left in New Mexico, the majority of their army is still engaged in the south. If there is any time to resist, it is now."

"I agree," Tomasito said. "I've already discussed these issues with our Pueblo elders."

"We have most of Taos on our side," Herrera added.

Jesús raised an eyebrow. "*Most?* Not *all?*"

"*No,*" said Herrera. "There are those who collaborate with the americanos."

Antonio felt his concerns about disunity returning. He also recalled Don Juan Chávez, the rico from Santa Fe, who had recently been appointed Lieutenant Governor by the American authorities; Chávez's acceptance of the post had earned him so many enemies that he was now forced to take a bodyguard wherever he went.

"In any event," said Tomasito, "we must set a date for action."

"We need time," said Herrera, "but we can't wait too long. The americanos are rapidly tightening their grip."

Jesús suggested, "Sometime in December?"

Tomasito nodded approvingly. "In about a month and a half. Yes, that might offer us enough time to plan and to coordinate with the other pueblos and villages of the north."

Antonio felt an adrenaline rush as he listened. What had seemed impossible now seemed real. Could such a revolt succeed? The risks were many.

When Jesús and Antonio left the pueblo, the sun had begun to set; the Sangre de Cristo Mountains to the east were already fading into the darkness.

Perhaps, thought Antonio, *what really matters is that we try . . . that we make the effort to expel the americanos from our land.*

CHAPTER XV

Elena stood beside her horse and pulled her sparse clothing tighter around her body. The day was cool. A strong gust of wind blew across the open grassland; it carried a painful chill, but she welcomed it. It soothed her exhaustion somewhat.

A mass of dark gray clouds was rolling in from the east. *The land of the Tejanos,* she thought, as she looked at the horizon beneath the clouds. Fear, exhaustion, and homesickness had taken their toll. *I can't do this anymore. I can't go on.*

Her captors milled nearby as the group rested from the long hard ride. Russell walked toward her and grasped the bridle rein of the horse. He stroked the animal gently.

"You're riding a good horse here," he said, offering her his canteen. Her bound wrists fumbled with it.

Russell shrugged and cut her hands free. "I don't think you'll be going anywhere," he said, "not in this country anyway."

Elena took the canteen from him and sipped the water.

Calhoun stood nearby, chewing the tobacco McNally had stolen from the Indian. He smirked at Russell. "You're treating that pretty young thing mighty nice, Captain."

"You'll be minding your own business," Russell said firmly.

Elena handed the canteen back to Russell. Eyeing Calhoun warily, she backed away.

"So how much do you reckon we'll get for that girl in Dallas?" Calhoun asked.

"Don't know exactly," Russell said.

"Fifty dollars?"

Russell did not answer.

"A hundred dollars? What do you think a fine woman like that is worth? I'm just curious, Captain. I just want to know what I'm risking my life for here."

"You should have thought of that back in New Mexico territory. If you'd just let things be at that ranch, we wouldn't be dragging this girl along and worrying about who might be looking for us."

"You have no right to keep a man from having his due."

Russell paused and then walked toward Calhoun. He stared directly into Calhoun's eyes. "Let's get one thing clear, J. D. You don't decide what your dues are as a Ranger. You're not in charge of this group. You're here to follow my orders. Understand?"

Preacher Smith broke in from behind. "Captain, you two ought to stop your bickering. We have another problem now."

Russell frowned. "What are you talking about?"

"Look," Smith said, pointing toward the Mexican girl's horse.

The horse stood by itself. The girl was gone.

When Jesús and Antonio had returned to the trading post after that long-ago meeting at the pueblo, they had found Felipe sitting at a wooden table at the back of the barroom. He had closed the trading post an hour earlier. The scent of alcohol from several open beer bottles, and of corn from an open bin of maize, filled the air.

Antonio persuaded his brother to help clean the bar

and restock the wooden shelves with dry goods, then to have a drink of whiskey.

Felipe stayed depressed. Day and night he seemed unable to think of anything except his beloved Petra. He talked constantly of her kisses, her tenderness, and the plans and dreams they had discussed during the short time they were together.

Antonio finally convinced Felipe to return to work, to keep his mind and body occupied. Felipe's duties at the trading post did seem to turn his thoughts away from his sorrow, if only for a few hours at a time.

Felipe also took a strong interest in the imminent rebellion. He now joined Antonio, Jesús, Tomasito, Cortez, and Herrera in regular nighttime meetings, often at the trading post itself. The American army and newcomers continued to bully the longtime residents of Taos and the pueblo, and the whole area lay under a blanket of tension and anger. The situation had become a pressure cooker, ready to explode.

"I've just returned from a meeting with Tomasito and the others," Jesús said one night, as he joined Felipe and Antonio at the trading post. "We've moved the starting date for the resistance farther back."

Antonio was surprised. "Why?"

"We need more time to plan and organize."

Felipe asked, "When?"

"December twenty-fifth," said Jesús. "La Navidad. We hope to catch the gringos by surprise."

Antonio poured a cup of whiskey and handed it to Jesús.

"Gracias," Jesús said. He swallowed quickly and smacked his lips, then looked sympathetically at Felipe. "How are you doing, my boy?"

"I am told life goes on . . . that I have to accept Petra's fate . . . and *my* fate."

"There is wisdom in those words, Felipe. You have to ask yourself, what would Petra have wanted?"

"For us to survive. . . ."

"No," Jesús said. "Not merely to survive, but to *live*. My heart aches for my daughter every day, but it also burns with anger and passion and, yes, *revenge*."

As Felipe took another sip of whiskey, the trading post's outside door crashed open. Pablo Herrera raced inside, shaking visibly and breathing hard. Antonio stood up and motioned for Herrera to sit down.

"No, thank you." Their visitor remained standing, leaning with one hand braced against the table. Antonio turned to close the door.

Jesús stared at the newcomer. "What is wrong?"

"I don't have much time," Herrera gasped.

"Time for what?"

"I've come to warn you."

"Warn us of what?" asked Jesús. His eyes widened. "What is the problem, Pablo?"

"We've been betrayed."

The room fell deathly quiet. Felipe wore the expression of a man who had received a final, fatal blow.

Pablo continued, "Someone has informed the americanos of our plans. Their soldiers are already searching Taos and making arrests. Tomasito sent me to warn you and your family."

"Where is Tomasito now?" Jesús asked.

"He and his puebleño followers have fled to the mountains."

"And Cortez?"

"Mañuel Cortez is also with Tomasito. I'll be riding to join them as soon as I leave here."

"Do you know who betrayed us, Pablo?"

"Who can say? It is suspected that Don Juan Chávez from Santa Fe was aware of our plans. Half the leadership of Taos certainly knew, and many of them stand to lose wealth and power if things change again. Or word might have leaked out in the gambling dens of Doña Tules. It really doesn't matter. What does matter is that you must leave Taos at once."

"But have we been implicated?" Jesús asked.

Pablo thought for a moment. "You three only met with Tomasito and Cortez and me. Tomasito and Cortez are both gone, and I'll be leaving as well. As far as I know, few other conspirators are definitely aware of your involvement. It's possible you might escape suspicion." Pablo shook his head. "Still, I urge you to leave."

"I can't. This is my home."

"It must be your decision," said Pablo, turning toward the door. "I wish you the best, my friends, but I must be on my way." He opened the door, letting a cold gust of air into the trading post. "Vaya con dios!" The door slammed behind him.

Antonio dropped into a chair and leaned toward the others. "We *should* leave Taos."

"No," said Jesús.

"But the soldiers. . . ." muttered Felipe.

"Even if they were at the door to take me away, I will *not* flee." Jesús poured a small amount of wine into a wooden cup and gulped it down. "You two, however, should go. You and María are still young enough to start new lives elsewhere. Go back to el Río Abajo and Atrisco."

Antonio looked grimly at Felipe. "Perhaps Jesús is right. We should return to Atrisco, at least for now."

Felipe was quiet for a moment and then shook his head slowly. "I won't leave either. How can I? Petra is buried here. This is my home, too."

"No," Antonio pleaded. "Petra would want you to live . . . to leave Taos and find a place to live your life in peace."

Felipe shrugged his shoulders helplessly. "How can there be peace anywhere in times like these?"

Antonio leaned forward and stared directly into Felipe's eyes. "What would Petra have really wanted? Be honest with yourself, my brother."

Suddenly, a rustling sound came from outside the trading post. The wooden door swung open wide. This time it was not Pablo Herrera who burst in, but two soldiers in blue uniforms. One held a rifle firmly in his hands; the other clutched a pistol.

The soldiers surveyed the room. "You the only ones here?" asked the one with the pistol.

Jesús nodded silently.

"Are you open?" the soldier asked.

Jesús remained quiet. The soldiers tensed.

"We're closed," Antonio said quickly.

The solider with the rifle lowered his weapon and strode toward the table. "Closed or not, we want a drink."

Antonio and Felipe stared at each other with stunned expressions.

"You want a . . . drink?" asked Antonio in Spanish.

"Don't you people understand English?"

Antonio switched to their language. "I speak a little."

"Well, you'd best not be speaking that Injun talk around us Americans." Most americanos used the word "Injun" to refer to any language other than English.

"Just get your ass up and get us a drink," the soldier said. "We'll take some of that same wine you're drinking there."

Antonio smiled weakly, and rose from his chair to walk to the bar. It seemed that his family was not under suspicion after all; these soldiers had certainly not come to arrest anyone. *It looks as if we won't have to leave Taos,* Antonio thought as he poured drinks for the soldiers.

Elena panted frantically as she struggled into a grove of large shrubs. Thorns slashed her face and arms, and she bit her lip, forcing herself not to cry out from the pain. The men had already realized their captive had escaped; she could hear them shouting in the distance.

"She went that way!" one of the Tejanos yelled.

Another voice: "No, I think it was the other way."

At least they were sufficiently confused that they might not know where to look for her. Elena crouched beneath the top of the shrubbery, taking a few seconds to catch her breath. *What am I to do now?*

Then she heard some of the voices heading in her direction. She poked her head through a gap in the undergrowth.

Only about a hundred feet from her stood the large obnoxious Tejano she feared the most, the one they called "Jay Dee." Russell, the only one who had shown her any sympathy, was nowhere to be seen.

Elena glanced carefully behind her. The bushes where she crouched grew at the bottom of a group of ridges. More shrubs and large weeds grew at the top of the ridges. If she could make it up there, it might offer a better hiding place. But the only visible trail up was bare, mainly rock and dirt. Could she take the risk of running out into the open, where she might easily be spotted?

Elena looked up at the gathering clouds. The surrounding landscape seemed to become darker with every minute. Wind kicked the dust into swirling eddies and dancing parabolas. Then the first drops of rain hit her skin.

The big Texan muttered a curse and started away from the bushes. She saw him join some of the others farther down the bases of the ridges. None of the men looked in her direction.

Elena felt rising panic, like some uncontrollable force, urging her to move. She scrambled back through the brush on her hands and knees, reached the edge of the nearest ridge, and risked a quick look back at the men. The increasing rain and wind obscured her view of them.

She stood up as high as she dared and stumbled up the steep incline. A strong scent of ozone hung in the air. Heavy drops of rain splattered her face.

She wiped the water from her eyes and struggled on, falling twice before reaching the top. Finally on the crest of the ridge, she stood up slightly and looked back. The men, still faintly visible through the rain, showed no sign of having seen her. They were searching among the boulders at the base of the ridge.

Elena felt safer. She dropped back to her knees and crawled away from the edge of the ridge until she was sure the men would not see her when she stood up. Then she surveyed the broad plain of brush and mesquite that lay ahead of her. In the distance, where the plain met the western horizon, three large mesas protruded into the dark sky.

I can make it there, she thought. She jumped up and ran toward the distant mesas, which seemed to call to her as if personally offering her a refuge.

She got only a few hundred yards before someone grabbed her shoulders from behind.

"No!" she screamed. She twisted violently, breaking

the man's grip, but stumbling in the process. She landed hard on the ground and looked up in terror at the man leaning over her.

It was Russell. He bent to grip her upper arms as she struggled to rise. "Take it easy," he said, holding her in a kneeling position.

Elena began to sob uncontrollably. He stared at her for a long moment, as if wondering whether he should have let her go.

Finally he shook his head sadly. "I'm sorry. I can't let you try to make it on your own out there. We're too far into Comanche country, and we're being followed."

Elena could answer him only with a fresh burst of tears.

Russell took her hand and gently pulled her to her feet. "Believe me, I'm sorry. This is the best I can do. At the moment, it's for your own good."

He pointed back toward the base of the ridge. "Let's go."

Elena knew she had no choice.

CHAPTER XVI

After the first wave of arrests in Taos, Antonio had sent María to stay with his family in Atrisco. She had begged him to come with her, but as long as Jesús and Felipe remained to run the trading post, Antonio felt a sense of obligation to them. Besides, none of the family had been questioned or otherwise implicated in planning the rebellion. Antonio did promise María that he would come to see her in a month or so.

By late December, tensions between the nuevomexicanos and the americanos were worse than ever. While most of the leaders of the resistance had escaped and gone into hiding—Tomasito and Mañuel Cortez were suspected to be in the Sangre de Cristo Mountains, while Pablo Herrera was rumored to have taken refuge with the Jemez Indians—the soldiers and the sheriff's office continued to arrest suspected troublemakers. The harder the authorities tried to crack down, the greater the Mexican community's resentment became.

Things were no better in the Taos Pueblo. The American army continued to intimidate the local population and appropriate winter stores of grain, fueling an explosive cauldron of bad feelings. The entire region had become a tinderbox, ready to ignite with the slightest flicker from a smoldering ember.

After one arrest of three Taos Indians on obviously trumped-up charges—Sheriff Lee was apparently under pressure from the governor to root out additional information about possible insurrection—both villagers and Indians began to talk openly about attacking the jail and freeing the captives. The atmosphere had become so hostile that Lee was rumored to fear for his life. One night, he left for Santa Fe to meet with Bent, who now occupied the former Palace of the Governors.

Two days later, Antonio and Jesús were closing

down the trading post for the evening, Felipe rushed inside. "Something is happening across the plaza."

Antonio ran to the door. In the dim red glow of the setting sun, a crowd could be seen forming in front of the jail. "What is it?"

"Bent has returned to Taos," Felipe said.

"What? Is he mad? Doesn't he know how the people here feel about him?"

"He apparently came because of the trouble here, but seems to believe he can handle the situation by himself. He was repeatedly warned by the Americans in Santa Fe not to come to Taos, but he ignored them. He's home now with his wife; he arrived this afternoon."

"Did he bring more soldiers?"

"None. Word has it that the authorities in Santa Fe urged him to take a military escort, but he refused."

Antonio was amazed at Bent's arrogance. Apparently the governor still thought of the nuevomexicanos as "children" and still assumed they would be easy to control. *How can anyone so underestimate the temperament of the people?*

Jesús moved to the open doorway and stared into the gathering night. "This is not good," he muttered. "That crowd is growing by the minute."

"It started about half an hour ago," Felipe said. "Some Indians from the Pueblo stormed the jail, demanding that Lee release the Indian prisoners. He's held the protestors off so far, but they're getting angrier and angrier. And many of our local villagers

176

have now joined the pueblenos in their demands."

Jesús grabbed his pistol and his heavy wool overcoat. They left the trading post and made their way across the plaza, past the tall wooden flagpole where the American flag still flew.

Well over a hundred Taos villagers and Pueblo Indians surrounded the jail. Antonio recognized many of them from visits to the trading post. Several people held torches or lanterns.

Lee stood at the jail doorway clutching a rifle. His face was pale and drenched in perspiration as he faced the angry throng. The crowd was clearly incensed, but it had not quite reached the furor of an angry mob. If anything, those gathered about the small adobe building seemed to be deliberately maintaining a certain amount of patience and dignity. Perhaps there was also a sense of hopelessness and despair in the atmosphere.

"Let our friends go!" a Taos Indian shouted.

"You have no right to hold them," a Taos villager added.

By now the sun had dipped completely below the horizon.

Another man, holding a pistol, stepped out of the jail building and stood next to Lee. Antonio recognized the newcomer as Cornelio Vigil, a local Taoseño and a frequent customer of the trading post. Vigil had recently been appointed prefect of Taos by the occupying forces.

A knot formed in Antonio's stomach as he remembered his last visit to the jail. Petra's murderers had never been brought to justice. Everyone was sure of the culprits—three soldiers who had conveniently been "transferred" from Taos to Santa Fe shortly after the crime. The American army had ignored justice to stand by its own.

"Your Indian friends will be held here," Lee told the crowd.

More shouts of "Let them go!" echoed across the plaza.

"Tell us why they're being held!" someone demanded.

"I don't owe any of you an explanation. Now go back to your homes."

"You have no warrant . . . you have no charges!"

"Please . . . go home!"

"Not until you free those men."

Lee's face wore the despairing expression of a man who realized not only that the situation was out of his control, but that he wasn't even sure where he stood on it. He threw up his hands. "All right. You can take your friends with you, if you'll just leave."

A collective sigh of relief rose from the crowd. Antonio felt the tension in his chest ease.

Jesús also relaxed visibly. "Lee's not stupid," he said. "Surely he knows what he's up against. By the same token, now is not the time for us to challenge the authorities. With half our leadership in hiding, we don't have the organization anymore."

But as the sheriff turned toward the jail entrance, Cornelio Vigil shoved him back and said loudly enough for everyone to hear, "Those Indians are *not* going anywhere. They stay *here*. Is that understood?"

A fresh wave of fury swept through the crowd.

"Damn you, Vigil!" a voice yelled.

Vigil gripped his pistol tightly and waved it at the crowd. "All of you, get the hell out of here!"

A shot rang out—not from Vigil's pistol, but from somewhere in the crowd. Vigil staggered back, his pistol tumbling from his hand. A rush of blood spurted from his chest and soaked his shirt. Slowly his legs collapsed and he sank to the ground.

As if that were a signal, the whole crowd exploded forward, screaming in an unstoppable release of pent-up rage. Some brandished knives or pistols. A few held picks or axes. Antonio stared, paralyzed, as the mob collided with Sheriff Lee and forced him back into the adobe building, yelling and shouting in a release of pent-up rage. Some were brandishing knives and pistols. The crowd forced Lee into the jail. Antonio could not make out what was occurring inside the building. He heard a scream, then came a moment's silence, followed by jubilant cheers.

Antonio, Felipe, and Jesús elbowed their way through the throng of people and into the jail. Barely inside the entrance, the sheriff lay dead across the wooden floorboards, his body drenched with blood from multiple stab wounds, his eyes and mouth still wide open in an expression of shock.

Antonio looked toward the cheering crowd at his left. The jail cell stood open and an enthusiastic crowd surrounded the newly released Indian prisoners. It had all taken less than five minutes.

Nor was it over. By the time Antonio fought his way out of the jail and back into the plaza, several men had surrounded the flagpole and were pulling down the hated American flag. Felipe pushed to Antonio's side; Jesús was nowhere in sight.

Others of the crowd, which had grown to well over two hundred angry people, raced from the plaza to a small adobe building several streets away. A tall bearded man walked out of the building, his expression one of indignant anger.

"Armstrong," Antonio said to Felipe.

"The lawyer?"

Antonio nodded.

Armstrong was staring incredulously at the crowd. "What is going on here? What is the meaning of this?"

Several men seized him and dragged him away from the building. Armstrong struggled furiously. "You goddamned greasers!"

Several enraged people, women as well as men, rushed forward and began tearing at the lawyer's clothes, stripping him naked.

Several voices yelled, "Kill the americanos!"

Antonio heard Armstrong's shouts of anger change to pleas for mercy as the lawyer was dragged through the dirt streets back to the plaza. Several people drew knives as Armstrong was forced to the ground. Moments later, he lay dead in his own blood, his scalp sliced from his head.

Antonio and Felipe stood helpless. They felt sickened by the events unfolding before their eyes, but they also could not help but think of Petra and the indignities suffered by her and so many of their fellow nuevomexicanos since the occupation by the American army.

Antonio heard the voices of men—apparently leaders of the crowd—ordering the others to "spare the women and children." Suddenly he realized that, despite the fever-pitched emotions of the crowd, this was not merely an angry mob killing at random. This crowd was driven by a controlled purpose.

Then he heard several people shout the name "Bent."

"Bent must know by now what is happening here. He must have barricaded himself in his house," Felipe said.

Antonio nodded. "Bent's home is like a fortress. He might be able to hold out until reinforcements arrive from Santa Fe."

The crowd was now moving along a winding dirt road. After several miles, they stopped in front of a large adobe hacienda—Bent's hacienda. "Come out, gringo!" several voices shouted.

The doors of the hacienda were flung open and the crowd momentarily quieted. Bent stepped out, grown fatter from luxury since Antonio had last seen him.

Bent opened his hands as if expecting to be greeted by the crowd. "My children," he said. "Go home. It is late in the evening."

"*You* go home, gringo!" someone shouted.

"Leave our land!" added another.

Bent stepped forward and raised his head haughtily. "Surely you know your resistance is useless. Even now, a mighty American army is moving toward Taos."

Antonio suspected Bent was lying—not that even an oncoming army would have been likely to quell the crowd's anger at that moment. Bent's arrogance was truly unbelievable. Any man with common sense would have stayed in the hacienda, or at least armed himself before coming out. But even in the face of all that had happened, Bent still seemed to believe he could placate any Mexican with his mere presence.

"Leave your weapons here and return to your homes," Bent insisted.

He was answered by the snap of a bowstring from somewhere in the crowd. An arrow arched into the air, caught the moonlight for a second, and then struck Bent in the shoulder. He fell backward, yelling in pain.

"Kill him!" the crowd screamed.

Felipe bolted forward from Antonio's side as the mob rushed toward Bent, who finally seemed to realize that his words had fallen on deaf ears. He turned and ran back toward the front door of his hacienda, the arrow still lodged in his shoulder. Swept along by the enraged crowd, Antonio felt the ground tremble, and for a brief moment he felt himself back on the open plain of the Llano Estacado, closing in on a herd of roaring buffalo.

He saw Bent stumble back inside, too late to close the door against the rush of the crowd. Knife blades flashed in the air. Minutes later, Antonio saw Bent's scalped and severed head raised and mounted on a pike. The crowd paraded their grisly trophy back to the plaza and stood it next to the flagpole. Like the sudden roar of a dormant volcano, the rebellion to expel the americanos from el Reyno had begun.

Now, years later, Antonio watched a pebble-sized *perrodo* crawling across the dirt in front of him. *You're at home here on the llano, little insect,* he thought as the black stinkbug made its way into a thatch of dry twigs. *If only Elena were so lucky.*

The sun was blazing overhead. Antonio lay flat on his stomach and wiped sweat from his forehead as he peered through his field glasses at the wide canyon ahead.

From his position on a rocky overlook, Antonio watched the Indian warriors riding down the left side of the canyon ahead. Farther ahead, the walls of the canyon gradually diminished and opened into a broad dry expanse. Then Antonio saw the other group of riders, moving out onto the plain.

Although this group was too far away for Antonio to make out more than colors and outlines, his heart beat faster as he recognized one of them as a woman. *Elena. It must be.*

Although Antonio was not sure why these *Rinches*—known for their brutality toward Mexicans—had kept his daughter alive, he was relieved to know she was safe. At least for the moment. But now she was in danger not only from the Tejanos, but also from the Comanches, who were no doubt trailing the Tejanos to take revenge for the other Indian's death. Antonio would hardly blame the Indians if they killed the raiders, but if Elena was caught with the Tejano group, it was unlikely the Indians would spare her.

Antonio returned to his horse and opened the leather satchel hanging from the saddle. He removed his flint and his steel *chispa* and then scanned the immediate surroundings. A group of large dry mesquite bushes clung to the edge of the cliff. Antonio quickly gathered several dead branches and piled them beside one of the bushes. Then he began scraping the flint against the chispa. The first sparks quickly dissipated.

Finally, a small dancing flame formed, caught, and grew into a small fire. Antonio threw some additional dry grass onto the fire and let the bush itself start burning, sending a black plume of smoke into the sky. Then he swung back onto his horse and galloped off in the direction the Tejanos were going.

Russell glanced back over his shoulder and suddenly brought his horse to a halt at the sight of the smoke rising from the distant canyon wall. He squinted in the bright sun and surveyed the endless blue horizons. Not a cloud in the sky.

The rest of the party stopped and followed Russell's gaze to the distant smoke.

"Couldn't be natural," Smith said.

"My thoughts exactly." Russell glanced back at Elena, whose horse was trailing directly behind him—in fact, was now tied to his own horse with a rope connecting the bridles. A shorter rope, leaving her just enough freedom of movement to control her horse's reins, again bound her wrists.

Calhoun suddenly pointed at the side of the canyon opposite the smoke. "Look up there." From this distance, they could barely make out four small figures on horseback, creeping along the canyon wall. "Injuns."

Smith shot Calhoun a disgusted glance. "*Your* Injuns, J. D."

Calhoun shrugged. "Ain't no matter."

"You won't be saying *no matter* if they get hold of you." Russell turned to the other Rangers. "But it's going to take them a while to get through that canyon. If we move fast, we might be able to lose them."

The other men nodded.

Russell shouted, "Move out!" and spurred his horse into a gallop. The rest of the party raced after him, out across the open plain.

CHAPTER XVII

In the days following the Taos uprising, Mañuel Cortez had returned from the Sangre de Cristo Mountains. A combination of hope and fear had permeated both the village of Taos and the nearby pueblo. There were rumors that the Americans had fled New Mexico; there were also rumors that a large American army had been dispatched from St. Louis to crush the rebellion.

Cortez gathered his followers in Taos, which was celebrating its freedom. He then traveled throughout the surrounding countryside to rally support, stirring up the men of Mora and the Taos valley and attacking the few Americans living in the rural areas.

News of the rebellion soon reached Santa Fe, and the American occupying force immediately sent a request for reinforcements to their army. Few reinforcements were immediately available, however; the larger force was still engaged in México and California. So the Americans in Santa Fe began forming regiments of their own, consisting of the few remaining soldiers in the territory and of recently arrived immigrants from the east, most of whom were living in and around Santa Fe. These regiments consisted mostly of the "Missouri Volunteers" and of mountain men like Bent, many of whom vowed to scalp any Mexican they came across. The army tortured and hanged many a civilian, men and women alike, as they moved north from Santa Fe.

They encountered far heavier resistance than expected, notably at Santa Cruz de la Canada. In their contempt for the humble nuevomexicanos, the Americans had misjudged how rage can fuel resistance. The ragtag army of nuevomexicanos, formed from the surrounding villages, fought a pitched battle for hours.

Finally, the small rebel regiment was forced to disperse with heavy casualties. The Americans continued north toward Taos.

In the early morning hours, Antonio sat next to Felipe inside the heavily fortified Taos Pueblo church. An army of some three hundred American soldiers was massed outside, prepared for the impending assault. Howitzers and other heavy artillery ringed the building. The scent of blood and sweat hovered inside.

Antonio and Felipe had spent the previous evening with six hundred other men, holed up in the Sangre de Cristo Mountains, fighting the Americans. The battle raged throughout the night, but the American army's superior weapons finally won out over the nuevomexicanos, who fought mainly with bows, arrows, spears, and old Spanish muskets. The nuevomexicano rebels, having suffered heavy losses, had now retreated to the temporary safety of the Taos Indian Pueblo.

When the army of blue-uniformed soldiers marched into Taos, Antonio and Felipe had at first joined their fellow rebels in hand-to-hand combat outside the Taos church. But the invaders' arms were too difficult to withstand, and soon the hundred or so defenders had taken refuge in the fortified adobe building.

Jesús Aguírre had made his way to the church earlier. He rallied the rebels inside, helping out in any way he could. A young Pueblo Indian woman offered a cup of water to Antonio and then to Felipe. Antonio gulped feverishly and then handed the cup to his brother.

"Thank you," Felipe said, gazing at the beautiful woman in admiration. Then a flush of guilt crossed his face.

Antonio smiled weakly. "It's human nature, my brother, even in a holy place like this."

"Padre Martinez would call it a sin," Felipe said.

Antonio shook his head. "Somehow I doubt God would punish us for something that is truly human."

"Perhaps you're right," said Felipe. "But I have to wonder where God is in these times."

The roar of cannons suddenly shook the entire building. Dirt and wood fell from the ceiling, scattering dust and rocks throughout the room. Antonio heard several women scream and looked up to see Tomasito, the Taos Indian leader, scampering from one side of the church interior to the other.

Jesús rushed up to Antonio and Felipe. "We have no more weapons, except these." He handed them two bows and a quiver of arrows.

"Where are the guns?" asked Felipe.

"This is all we have," said Jesús. "I'm sorry."

Another explosion bellowed, and the church shook again.

"How long can we hold out?" Antonio asked.

"As long as these walls stand, so can we." Jesús glanced at the church altar where a large crucifix, a bulto, and several wooden santos stood silently against a backdrop of mud plaster and adobe. "We have fought valiantly," he told Antonio and Felipe. "We have done the best that we could."

Antonio sighed. "If only we could have done more."

Felipe said with a touch of sadness, "The nuevomexicanos have fought in vain. The americanos are a conquering army, and we are a conquered people. And did my Petra ever receive justice?"

Jesús smiled. "Some kind of justice is served by all of this, I suppose. Promise me one thing," he added, looking at Antonio. "If you manage to survive, take care of your own; take care of my daughter."

Antonio nodded. "I will."

Shouts in English could now be heard outside the church. The cannons had ceased firing, at least for the moment. A muffled scraping sounded from Antonio's immediate left, near one of the church walls. "What are they doing?"

Suddenly a small portion of the wall gave way, forming a gap in the adobe bricks—just wide enough for the barrel of a cannon.

"Back!" Jesús screamed.

Antonio and Felipe jumped away as a sudden roar echoed through the interior of the church. For a moment Antonio heard only silence, followed by a ringing in his ears. Thick black smoke filled the air as the church rattled. Antonio struggled to his feet. Dead bodies lay everywhere: some leaning against the old wooden pews; some sprawled on the floor.

The ceiling had begun to collapse. Supporting vigas dropped from the roof and crashed to the floor. As the dust settled, Antonio heard a steady clamor just beyond the church doors and realized that the soldiers were about to break through.

He turned to see Jesús lying face down on the floor in a pool of blood. The old man's legs had been completely severed from his body. Antonio's stomach lurched. He bent over his father-in-law. Jesús was dead.

Antonio fought back tears. There would be time for grieving later. His eyes swept around the interior of the church. He saw still more bodies and heard the moans of the wounded.

"Ayúdame . . ." several voices pleaded.

Then a faint voice called, "Antonio."

"Felipe!" Antonio saw his brother lying on the ground near an alcove where rows of lit candles had once stood. He raced over and helped Felipe sit up.

Some of the survivors were fleeing through a small door at the rear of the church. "We have to escape," Antonio said.

Felipe moaned. "I can't move my leg."

Antonio pressed on the upper part of Felipe's left leg.

Felipe yelled.

"We must leave now!" Antonio insisted.

"No . . . you go . . . leave me here."

"But, Felipe. . . ."

"Leave me here now!"

"I can't."

"Remember what you promised Jesús. *You* have María to look after."

The broad wooden church doors gave way. Blue uniformed soldiers pushed the large doors open and rushed in.

The few remaining rebels attacked the soldiers with bare hands and knives. The soldiers retaliated with bullets.

"Go. . . ." Felipe said.

Antonio darted toward the back door, coughing from the thick smoke and dust. He broke into the cold January air and dashed for the nearby home of a Pueblo Indian family he knew. There, he hid in a small alcove from which he was able to look out at the church, through a small gap in the walls.

He could see the blue-uniformed Americans pulling dead bodies from the ruined church; Antonio recognized one as the Indian leader Tomasito. Other rebel fighters, including Felipe, were dragged out still alive. One of the survivors was Pablo Herrera, who seemed uninjured and now stood with his hands tied behind his back. A group of American soldiers marched Herrera to a tall álamo and tied a rope around his neck. After hanging Pablo from the tree, the soldiers laughed and spat at his body.

By dusk, most of the American soldiers had left the pueblo, after establishing a curfew and martial law. Similar restrictions were placed on the village of Taos, where the majority of the soldiers went.

Shortly after dark, Antonio's hosts told him it was safer for him to leave the pueblo. They gave him a large beaver skin overcoat and a small sack of carne seca and tortillas. He fled eastward toward the rocky foothills of the nearby Sangre de Cristo Mountains, where he found a pile of fallen boulders that formed a cave-like shelter. He remained there for two days, managing to make his meager supply of food last for the interval.

On the third day, Antonio risked returning to Taos. The weather was bitterly cold, which gave him an excuse to keep his face hidden in his overcoat. American soldiers were everywhere, but none of them showed any signs of recognizing him as a rebel. Jesús Aguírre's trading post was closed, probably permanently.

The American flag flew once again over the Taos plaza, where several hundred people were gathered. Except for a few jubilant gringos, most of the crowd went about with somber faces and subdued voices. Several people were sobbing audibly.

A wooden gallows, hastily constructed from two wooden poles and a horizontal support, stood in front of the American jail. Soldiers, obviously nervous, stood on guard. A cannon was mounted on the roof of the jail.

Then Antonio saw the row of prisoners being led in chains to the gallows. He counted twenty-four, most of whom he knew. Some were well-respected community leaders; many were young. Antonio stood silently as he watched them approach. *Mañuel Miera . . . Jose Mañuel Garcia . . . Pedro Lucero . . . Isidor Romero . . . patriots, all of them.*

Antonio felt a wrenching pain in his heart as he noticed one man limping at the end of the line. *Felipe.* Antonio's brother walked with his head hung low.

The soldiers unchained Felipe and the five prisoners immediately in front of him. To the beating of a drum, the men were herded onto a wagon. A mule dragged the wagon forward, stopping beneath the gallows from which hung six ropes.

The drum roll stopped and an American army officer stepped in front of the wagon. "By the order of the court of the territory of New Mexico, these men are to be executed as traitors to their country, the United States of America!"

Several shouts of "Hurrah!" came from the Anglos in the crowd. The Mexicans were silent.

Antonio caught a last glimpse of the blank stare on Felipe's face before black hoods were pulled over the prisoners' heads. Ropes were tightened about their necks. The drum roll began again and the wagon began to move forward.

Antonio forced himself to stand still and watch silently. It was all he could do for Felipe now, to stay there until the end.

Felipe's body writhed and jerked for what seemed an eternity. Finally, his body hung limply from the rope. The soldiers began to cut the corpses down as the next group of prisoners was forced to mount the wagon. A woman to Antonio's left clutched her baby and wept hysterically. Probably the wife of one of the executed men.

Tears streamed down Antonio's own face as he watched the wagon again approach the gallows. The scene played itself out four times, until the last body was removed from the makeshift gallows. A cheer bellowed from several American soldiers, and a gringo civilian shouted, "Tonight we celebrate this great victory!"

Antonio walked away, feelings of intense anger and sorrow tearing through his body. Part of him wanted to attack and kill the first American he came across. Another part wanted only to run away and hide and forget. Images of death burning into his mind, he left the village that same day and headed south toward Atrisco. He would never see Taos again.

I will not lose another loved one, Antonio vowed as he spurred his horse over a patch of light golden chamisa. The sagebrush was interspersed with a number of small cacti and large rocks.

Antonio's horse whinnied in frustration at the rough terrain. "Bueno," he whispered, easing it into a slow trot.

Behind him, the flames continued to rise into the sky. Antonio was sure that both the Indians and los Rinches had seen it. By alerting the Tejanos that they were being pursued, thus keeping the Indians from catching them by surprise, he hoped he had bought Elena some time.

Several yards from the fire, Antonio turned his horse behind a group of large boulders and came to a stop.

Through his field glasses, he saw the Indians looking in the direction of the black plume.

Good. They suspect they're being followed. Maybe they'll give up their pursuit of the Tejanos.

He turned his glasses in the direction of the Tejanos. They had considerably increased the distance between and were moving away at a strong gallop. Dust trailed behind their horses.

Losing sight of the Tejano riders as they merged into the horizon, Antonio glanced again at the Indians below and saw them reach the bottom of the canyon. "¡Ándale!" he shouted at the horse, urging it onto a side trail.

Although it had been years since Antonio had visited this part of the llano, he knew the terrain well. This place was *el cañon de la chamisa,* so known to the nuevomexicanos for the bountiful chamisa that grew at its rim. Antonio was sure he could pick up the Tejanos' trail once he was on the open plain. *It is merely a matter of time and patience,* he thought, recalling how he had learned to track and hunt game in his youth. A sentimental smile formed on his lips as he thought of how Tío Tomás had trained him. *If ever there was a natural tracker, it was Tomás.*

Still, Antonio was worried. He was now in the eastern recesses of the Llano Estacado. If the gringos continued in their current direction, they would come out of the unsettled llano onto the Texas flatlands in a few days, or a week at most. If they got Elena that far, there might be no hope of finding her.

CHAPTER XVIII

When Antonio had returned to Atrisco years earlier, little had changed. The old Alcalde mayor had been replaced by a gringo; a gringo sheriff had been installed; a new English-language newspaper was circulating in the area; and the small village to the east of Atrisco was now called Albuquerque instead of the original Spanish Alburquerque. The land itself, however, appeared essentially as it had for generations. The Sandía Mountains still rose majestically to the east; to the west, three small dormant volcanoes still sat stoically above an ancient lava flow that had formed a series of black cliffs. The Río Abajo and the surrounding Spanish-speaking communities and Indian Pueblos were much the same as Antonio remembered; so were the small farms and ranchitos that hugged the eastern and western Río Grand Bosque, from the northern reaches of Bernalillo and Algodones and southward to Socorro. Except for the occasional raid by Apaches or Navajos, most of the communities of the Río Abajo continued as they had for generations.

Within a few years, however, even this area was showing symptoms of change.

Antonio's father, Francisco, had died—of a broken heart, Antonio was convinced—soon after Antonio brought the news about Felipe. Within a year, Antonio's mother, María Elena, also passed away. Not too long afterward, the old Cibolero Tío Tomás joined his brother and sister-in-law.

Antonio was tired of violence and now wanted only to be a peaceful farmer. He and María settled on a small parcel of land in Los Bacas with easy access to la acequia and the fresh waters of the Río Grande. Antonio planted fields of frijoles, chile verde, and maíz, as well as a small orchard of apples and pears. Now was the time for Antonio and María to begin raising a family. Soon their first child, Elena, was born.

Atrisco and Albuquerque remained small hamlets on the respective west and east banks of the Río Grande, still the home primarily of nuevomexicanos. But soon more newcomers began to arrive from the east, bringing their ways with them. Occasionally, a pobre americano wandered through Los Bacas and approached Antonio asking for a handout or food. Despite the anger Antonio still harbored toward the americanos, he could not make himself turn away any poor stranger who arrived barefoot and starving. Still, he suspected that the americanos ricos would not long be satisfied to leave these lands to the Mexican populace.

Sure enough, he soon began hearing stories of gringos using various legal and extralegal means to acquire rights to vast tracts of land throughout New Mexico. While the traditional Spanish and Mexican land grants had been formally acknowledged under the Treaty of Guadalupe Hidalgo that ended the war between México and the United States, the americanos routinely ignored the grants.

Traditionally, most of the land grants had held available pasture or open space for use by the entire community, and only the produce of the land was taxed by the Spanish and later, Mexican authorities. Under the new American laws, however, the land itself was taxed. Moreover, these laws were written in a foreign language, English, while the vast majority of the population spoke only Spanish. It was not long before the newcomers from the east began to use these new laws to dispossess the New Mexicans of their land.

Eight years after returning to Atrisco, Antonio had his first personal encounter with the new legal system imposed by the americanos. He and his family had settled into a comfortable pattern of life on their small ranchito near the Río Grande bosque: spring gave way to summer with its hot days in the fields; autumn arrived with its harvests, roasting green chile, matancias, and preparations for the winter; the cold of winter passed and yielded to the warmth of spring. For some time, Antonio hoped that the events of the outside world would pass him by for the rest of his life.

One fall afternoon, however, he was picking his crop of green chiles when he saw three gringos near the bosque of álamos at the edge of his ranchito. Everyone who lived in the area, including the few recently arrived Americans, knew each other, but these men were strangers.

Antonio studied the men as they approached along the long narrow dirt path from the opposite end of the field. Two of the men were dressed in the latest eastern fashions. The third man was dressed in buckskin clothing and had a white beard. He reminded Antonio of the self-styled mountain men back in Taos.

"How you doing?" the man in buckskins asked Antonio. "Habla inglés?"

Antonio nodded. "Yes."

"Mah name's Jake Walker." The man gestured toward his two companions. "These two gentlemen here recently arrived from Missouri. They're surveying New Mexico territory." The two men nodded at Antonio but did not offer to shake his hand. He sensed a hint of condescension in their manner.

"And your name is?" asked Walker.

"Antonio Baca."

"Mr. Baca," said the tall Easterner with the thin mustache and large blue eyes, "my name is Herbert Wellington. I'm an attorney. This is my business associate, Jeffrey Stevenson." Stevenson was a short and stocky man with a well-rounded belly.

"Mucho gusto," Antonio said suspiciously.

"You have a very nice spread here," Wellington said.

"Thank you."

"Yes, quite beautiful, particularly this time of the year." Stevenson smiled. "Plenty of water from the river and the irrigation canals. I did not realize such a verdant area could be found in this godforsaken desert. I was admiring your orchard and cottonwoods.

You have a virtual paradise here, Mr. Baca. I compliment you."

Antonio said nothing.

"Mr. Baca," Walker said, "these men are interested in buying land in this area."

Antonio shrugged. "That might be difficult. Everything as far as you can see from here is part of the Baca land grant. A league from here you'll find the same at Atrisco. The same is true up and down this valley. The land from here to the mountains belongs to the communities of Albuquerque, Los Gallegos, Los Padillas, and Alameda. It is not for sale."

"That is a shame because we think there is money to be made here. There is talk of a railroad coming this way soon," Stevenson said.

"This would also make fine dairy country," added Wellington. "Plenty of water to irrigate these fields."

"Perhaps you should look somewhere else for land," Antonio advised.

"We are willing to offer you a fair price for your property," said Stevenson. "We represent powerful business interests, from Santa Fe and the east, who want to see a railroad come through these parts."

"This land is *not* for sale. It's been in our family for generations. The Baca land grant was granted by the King of Spain over a hundred and fifty years ago."

"This is not Spain, and no longer México," Stevenson said.

"Thank you for your offer, but I'm not interested. And I can tell you that you'll find a similar sentiment among most of the surrounding communities."

"Very well," said Wellington. He turned to his companions. "Let's get going."

Antonio watched the strangers depart, and shook his head as he returned to gathering the chile verde. Somehow, he suspected he would be hearing of this again.

Russell and the preacher were out surveying the surrounding terrain. McNally poured himself a cup of coffee and walked past the Mexican girl, who sat on the dirt with her legs and arms bound. The other Rangers were tending to their horses.

Calhoun wandered over, muttering, "I'm tired of this crap. Not enough food and now the water's almost out."

"You signed up just like I did."

"No," said Calhoun. "My pa *volunteered* me."

"Your pa's some kind of rancher or a politician, right?"

"He's a rancher all right, but not a politician. You might say that he *owns* the politicians. Not to mention most of the countryside around Waco. He's a real hero, my pa is. Fought in the war against the Yankees and killed the last of the Injuns around Waco. Drove out the few Mexicans left and took it all for himself. Now he must have a million head of cattle on his land."

"Seems to me," said McNally, "that your pa ought to be able to make an example of Captain Russell for giving you such a hard time."

Calhoun placed a pinch of tobacco into his mouth

and looked bitterly at the girl. "Russell is a greaser lover. That's why he's keeping her alive."

"Well, the captain says we ought to be leaving this country soon. We should be seeing some settlements any time now."

"It's been a long time since I had a woman," Calhoun said. "I'm tired of waiting."

"A few more days," McNally said. "Just a couple of more days and you can have all the women you want. I'm sure there'll be plenty of whores for you once we reach the settlements."

"This senyorita here is my *reward*," said Calhoun, staring at Elena.

Disgusted by the expression on Calhoun's face, she turned her head away from him.

"What's the matter?" he snarled. "Ain't you ever been with a white man?" he shouted.

Elena began sobbing softly. She shrank back.

He walked up to her and began stroking her hair. "It's a crying shame," he whispered.

McNally grabbed Calhoun's shoulder. "Back off, J. D. We have enough trouble as it is after that dead Injun back there. Let's just get through this without upsetting the captain anymore."

"Captain Russell can just mind his own damned business."

"Listen, J. D.," McNally pleaded, "I just want to go home. Forget the Mexican girl. She's not worth the trouble. Understand what I'm telling you?" Calhoun snorted and turned away from the girl.

"God willing, we'll be home soon," said McNally. "You can let your pa deal with the captain then."

Antonio remembered that day years ago when the afternoon sun hung in the blue sky and the cottonwoods swayed gently in the soft wind. Most of the leaves were still green, although a few patches of golden yellow leaves suggested a possible early winter.

Antonio was picking maíz near the bosque. He stopped to savor the fresh air and watch a small deer scamper across the ranchito. Antonio had cleared most of the field over the last several days. The autumn harvest was plentiful, but that meant plenty of work to be done. Fortunately, it also meant a good winter. He and María should be able to sell some of the crop in Albuquerque and have enough left to feed the family until spring.

María, who had been washing clothes in a large tin pail outside their small adobe house, suddenly shouted for Antonio. He hurried toward the house to see five men approaching from the northern edge of the ranchito. Antonio recognized three of them as the strangers who had asked him about buying land, only a week earlier.

"Take the children inside," he called to María, and went to meet the visitors.

He now recognized the two men with Wellington, Stevenson, and Walker. They were the recently appointed americano sheriff of Albuquerque, and his deputy. The sheriff held a rifle, and the deputy a pistol.

"Mr. Baca," Stevenson said. "Good day."

Antonio eyed them suspiciously.

Wellington was holding several sheets of paper. He handed one sheet to Antonio. "This is a copy, Mr. Baca, of a claim that was recently filed with the authorities in Santa Fe."

Antonio looked at the paper. "Just what type of a *claim* is this?"

"It is a claim under federal law, and it has been duly recorded."

Antonio shrugged. "Yes, but a claim to *what?*"

"To this land, of course," said Stevenson. "As far as the law is concerned, you are a trespasser on *our* land, Mr. Baca, as are a number of your neighbors."

"You're not serious."

"We are *very* serious, Mr. Baca." Wellington handed Antonio the remaining sheets of paper. "I also advise you to take a look at these documents. These records indicate that this entire area is subject to back taxes."

"Taxes on what, may I ask?"

"On this land, Mr. Baca."

"We have never before received any notification about any taxes owed."

"That does not matter, Mr. Baca."

"¡Éstas son mis tierras!" Antonio shouted angrily. "Leave now!"

"I'm afraid that isn't possible, Mr. Baca."

"The claim is valid," the sheriff said. "As are the tax records." He raised his rifle and gestured toward the adobe house. "You'll have to vacate this property by tomorrow morning."

"I built that house with my own hands. These lands were granted to us by the King of Spain. And the treaty that gave this land to the United States also guaranteed the land grants. Your own military leaders posted the treaty throughout this territory after the war."

"Well, Baca, your king ain't here now," the sheriff said. "If you know what's good for you, you'll gather your family up and get out of here by tomorrow."

"I do not want any trouble," said Antonio. "I just want to be left alone on my own land."

"You can go somewhere else and be left alone," the sheriff said.

For how long? Antonio wondered. For a moment, he considered rushing into the house for his rifle. But most of his will to fight for what rightfully and legally belonged to him had died back in Taos. He sighed and let his shoulders slump.

Jake Walker spoke up. "Mr. Baca, I can help you pack your belongings."

"No," said Antonio.

"Well, in any event, Mr. Baca," Wellington said with a smile, "you should plan on being off our property by sunset tomorrow. Take what you can, but go. Is that understood?"

The five men turned and strolled away without waiting for an answer. Antonio flung the papers to the ground and trod on them as he stomped into the house.

María took the news stoically. "We must leave. We have little choice."

Antonio looked at his rifle. "Maybe not."

"I already have a dead sister, and you have a dead brother. I'm tired of so much death around us."

So the following day Antonio loaded his family, his few belongings, and as much of the crops as had been harvested onto a carreta, and drove away from their home of the past eight years. He refused to look back.

CHAPTER XIX

Kyle Adams had fallen behind the other horsemen. The captain had instructed Kyle to guard the rear as they rode through a countryside littered with large twisted boulders. "Stay alert," Russell had warned.

Kyle, however, was exhausted, and the oppressive late afternoon sun made him all the more drowsy and lethargic. His eyes became heavy, and he soon drifted into a stupor.

He suddenly snapped awake about half an hour later, to realize that he was alone in the wilderness. His horse had wandered away from the other riders, who were nowhere to be seen.

"Shit," he muttered, rubbing his blurry eyes and pulling his horse to a stop. He scanned his immediate surroundings and saw nothing alive, except several small lizards scampering over a nearby boulder. The sun continued to beat down. Kyle looked around nervously, unsettled and confused by the silence of the empty wilderness.

About a hundred yards away, Antonio gazed through his field glasses and saw the straggler awake from his doze. Antonio had drawn close to the Tejano party some six miles back to see this rider lagging behind the others. The rear horse was veering away to the north. The rider, apparently asleep, had made no effort to correct his mount.

Antonio had turned his own horse after the single rider. He remembered how the Ciboleros often searched for wayward buffalo during their seasonal hunts. This was no different from stalking a buffalo that had fallen away from the herd.

Now the lost rider dismounted, apparently taking stock of his surroundings. He put his canteen to his lips, then angrily threw it to the ground. The canteen bounced twice and clattered to a stop by the horse's hooves.

The young man seemed to reconsider. He picked up the canteen, then placed it to his lips again. *Must be out of water,* Antonio thought, *and hoping to suck out one last drop of moisture.*

Antonio tied his horse to a nearby bush and drew the knife from the sheath at his waist. Then he remembered the Cibolero lance hanging from the horse's saddle. He re-sheathed the knife and smiled as he reached for the lance. He was about to awaken his old friend from a long dormancy.

Antonio had not been the only land grant heir evicted from Los Bacas by the americano land speculators. Several of his cousins were also forced to leave their homes.

María and Antonio tried town life again for a time, settling in Santa Fe where Antonio found work as a teamster for a rich gringo merchant. This man lived in a large wooden mansion built in the strange architectural style brought by americanos from the east.

Although Antonio and his fellow nuevomexicanos were now legal citizens of the United States, they still thought of the gringos as the americanos—or as *bolillos* or *gavachos.* The newly arrived easterners also continued to regard the nuevomexicanos as a different people: Mexicans; Spaniards; or—when the americanos were feeling especially condescending—"greasers." Nor were most of the longstanding residents regarded as full citizens with equal rights. For the most part, they were treated as second-class citizens, as foreigners in their own land.

Most nuevomexicanos had always known poverty, but this condition increased in the years following the arrival of los americanos. As americano wealth and power grew, the vast majority of the native indios and mexicanos sank deeper into poverty. This problem was intensified by the better education enjoyed by the Anglos. A few native ricos sent their children to eastern schools, but the vast majority of nuevomexicanos remained illiterate or poorly educated. Some

American schools had been established in the territory of New Mexico, but these were run by Protestants from the east, who despised the Catholicism treasured in the heart and soul of most nuevomexicanos, and who discouraged, sometimes violently, the use of Spanish by New Mexican children.

Antonio did not want to raise his children in such an environment. He sensed what was happening. With the increasing arrival of the newcomers from the East, americano wealth and power grew, while that of the vast majority of the natives, both indios and mexicanos, rapidly decreased, resulting in impoverishment and resentment.

Antonio thought of taking the family south to México. Following the war with México, some New Mexicans refused to live in a homeland occupied by the foreign americanos and migrated south toward the northern provinces of México. *But* this *is my homeland,* Antonio thought. *I refuse to leave.*

Then an uncle of María's, Tío Armando, came to visit from his home in La Cuesta and told them that land was available below the sprawling Pecos wilderness southeast of Santa Fe. This rugged and isolated area was still subject to occasional Comanche or Apache raids, but it was far from gringo land interests. Antonio's family made the journey from Santa Fe the next spring. After two weeks of scouting for a new home, they found a small box canyon that seemed to offer the protection they sought from the outside world. A stream and several ojitos provided all the water they would need to plant fields and grow their crops.

They lived for a time in a cave at the edge of the canyon, while Antonio built a home of adobe and wood. He included a torreón for protection against Indian attacks. When he began planting and harvesting the crops, María worked alongside him. After several years, the fields were producing rich crops of corn, chile verde, and frijol. Antonio and María settled into life at their new el cañoncito de Los Bacas.

As time passed and the family grew, Antonio and María at last seemed to have found peace and permanence. But like an irresistible force of nature, events two thousand miles to the east would in time find their way there.

Kyle Adams stood next to his horse, staring into the surrounding wilderness. The jagged countryside seemed to stare back at him. *What the hell do I do now?*

To kill time while he thought, he pulled a small pouch of tobacco from his leather satchel. He placed it to his nose, savoring its scent. *Thank God J. D. killed that Injun and got us this tobacco,* he thought.

As he placed a chunk in his mouth, he suddenly felt something sharp prod him in the back. A voice commanded, "No se mueva!"

Kyle jumped and involuntarily swallowed his tobacco. He coughed violently. "Don't move," the voice ordered in English. "Raise your hands."

Kyle did as he was told.

"You may turn your head—but do it slowly!"

Kyle rotated his head cautiously and found himself staring into the dark eyes of a Mexican wielding a huge lance. Although Kyle was certain he had never seen the man before, some of the Mexican's features looked vaguely familiar. Kyle's eyes followed the lance and its bearer as they slid around from his back to his chest.

The Mexican glared at him. "You're with the Tejanos."

"*Tejanos?*"

"Texans."

"Yes," Kyle stammered.

"Where are you going?"

"We're headed down to Dallas and then to Waco."

The man nodded, as if recognizing the names of these small settlements.

"We're lawmen," Kyle added. "Rangers. Texas Rangers."

"Los Rinches," the man muttered. Although Kyle did not recognize the word, there was no mistaking the hostility with which it was uttered.

"Why were you in New Mexico Territory?" asked the man. "The Rangers have no authority there."

Kyle licked his lips. "We were looking for a horse thief."

"Traveling that far is going to a lot of trouble for a horse thief."

"He was also a colored man who'd been with a white woman."

"And did you find your thief?"

Kyle shook his head. "No. We lost his trail west of the panhandle."

"Comanchería," the man said, as if to himself. "How many ride with you?" he asked.

Kyle hesitated. The point of the lance instantly jabbed harder.

"Six," Kyle stammered. "Just six of us."

"Are you certain?"

"I wouldn't lie about that."

"But there is another with you, a girl?"

Kyle was surprised. "Well . . . yes." He felt beads of perspiration dripping into his eyes. "What do you want with me?" he groaned.

"With *you* . . . nothing."

"Then just let me be on my way. I don't mean any harm to you."

"I want my daughter back," the man said.

Kyle suddenly realized why this Mexican's facial features looked familiar. "I . . . I had nothing to do with it."

The man was silent, as if waiting for him to continue.

"You have to believe me," Kyle pleaded. "It was the others."

"Who?"

"The others . . . J. D."

"What reason do you people have for taking a young woman from her home and family?"

"It was J. D.'s idea, not mine."

"My son was shot. He is just a boy. What kind of animals would shoot a boy in the head?"

Kyle felt a lump form in his throat. "It wasn't me. Just let me be."

The man backed away one step and lowered the lance slightly. "And what are your companions planning to do with my daughter?"

"They're taking her to Dallas."

"What for?"

"To sell her."

The man's eyes blazed with shock and anger. "What do you mean, to *sell* her?"

"The captain said we could make some money down there in Dallas at the whorehouses. But I tell you, I had nothing to do with any of that. I'm just minding my own business, trying to get back home. That's all."

The man's eyes shifted slightly away, as if contemplating the enormity of it. Kyle snatched the opportunity and lunged for the pistol at his waist. He raised it to fire.

He never pulled the trigger. The lance thrust forward, plunging deep into the young Ranger's body. Kyle's head swam and the gun dropped into the dirt.

He felt his flesh tearing as the lance was pulled out. His body collapsed to the ground. Through a blurry haze, he saw the Mexican leaning over him. "Tell me about my daughter," the man demanded.

"Can't tell you any more," Kyle moaned. And as his mind drifted into darkness, he whispered, "But . . . you're just a *greaser.*"

When the Civil War had come to New Mexico, Antonio had had no intention of becoming involved in what he and most of his fellow New Mexicans had considered a foreign conflict. For six years, Antonio had farmed his ranchito in el cañoncito de Los Bacas, oblivious to the world outside the canyon. Except for an occasional trip to Las Vegas for supplies, he and his nearby neighbors lived their lives isolated from the larger events of the world.

Rarely was English heard in this part of New Mexico. Despite the continuing influx of immigrants from the East, Spanish remained the primary source of communication throughout the villages and countryside of the territory. News traveled slowly in this region, usually from La Cuesta up into the smaller villages and communities along the Río Pecos.

Antonio had no interest in americano politics or concerns. To him, the gray-uniformed soldiers were no different from their blue-clad counterparts. They were all simply gringos. While he had heard vague rumors that this was a fight to end slavery, and he certainly despised the cruelties of slavery, such events were far from his concern now.

So when a plea for volunteers to defend New Mexico against an invading column of Confederate soldiers finally made its way to the ranchito, Antonio hesitated. He could not stomach the idea of serving in the same army that had killed his brother and comrades in Taos years before. But when he learned that

Abraham Lincoln had appointed Estanislado Montoya as a general of New Mexico volunteers, Antonio began to reconsider. Montoya hailed from the Socorro region south of the Río Abajo.

Antonio respected Lincoln's opposition to slavery, and he knew that the tall awkward president he had seen in newspaper lithographs had opposed the war with México. And Estanislado Montoya himself was a nuevomexicano like Antonio; it was said that Montoya's family had lived here since the days of Oñate. But the factor that finally made up Antonio's mind was the news that the invading army of Confederate soldiers originated from Texas.

It did not surprise Antonio that the hated Texans had so eagerly joined the slave states in their attempt to dissolve the Union. If the Confederacy succeeded in its aims, if the Texans managed to conquer New Mexico, life would be even worse for his people than under the americanos. The Texas Confederates represented to him the worst of a power structure based on assumptions of racial superiority. He saw them as a serious threat not only to the New Mexican way of life but also to life itself.

Antonio felt that the isolation of el cañoncito de los Bacas would offer María and the children sufficient protection while he was away. And María knew how to shoot a rifle and fire a pistol. So Antonio left her to take care of things and rode northwest to Santa Fe.

Gringo and mexicano alike seemed under a pall of despair when he reached the capital in late February.

Antonio learned that the Union army had retreated north following their defeat at Valverde, south of Socorro. The Confederates had followed them northward and now occupied Albuquerque, which had been abandoned by federal forces.

Antonio found General Estanislado Montoya's regiment encamped at el paraje de las Golondrinas, south of Santa Fe. The army camp was spread out over several acres of land that had once served as a *paraje,* or stopping point, along the Camino Real. For two hundred years, caravans of teamsters and pack animals from Mexico City and Chihuahua had rested here.

The general was a round-faced man with jet black hair and sharp green eyes, and he looked more a foot soldier than a general. Indeed, Antonio soon found out that the soldiers held their general in high regard largely because the man was by no means regal. In this makeshift army, salutes and titles were rare. The general appeared tired and worn, but he was pleased to have additional volunteers from the surrounding countryside join his regiment.

Upon learning that Antonio had been a Cibolero, Montoya asked him to accompany a scouting patrol southwest from Santa Fe. For a day and a half, the small party traveled over the brown and green landscape along the Río Grande bosque. To the west the Jemez Mountains rose into the sky like jagged spires; to the southeast, the Sandía Mountains glinted in the sunlight.

The party eventually reached the hamlet of

Bernalillo. Late that afternoon, they camped atop a ridge to the west of the village. Antonio saw a long column of soldiers in gray uniforms moving north through the valley below, no doubt heading for the capital at Santa Fe. Once again a foreign army was advancing into the heart of el Reyno, and once again Antonio was about to take up arms against it.

CHAPTER XX

The early evening air was cool and refreshing after the long day of riding. Russell reined in his horse and gazed at the western horizon. Suddenly he noticed a blurry movement against the pink and yellow sunset. Russell signaled his men to wait, and watched cautiously as the silhouette of a lone horse became clear. Adams?

It looked like the right horse, but there was no rider in the saddle. The horse was heading in their general direction at a moderate gallop.

Preacher Smith leaned forward in his saddle. "It's Kyle's horse—but where's Kyle?"

Russell spurred his own horse forward to meet the approaching animal. As he drew close, he suddenly pulled up short with disbelief. Slowly, he reached out to take the other horse's reins and stared at the body tied atop the animal.

Russell shook his head. The horse *was* carrying Kyle Adams, after all—but Adams would never put a foot in a stirrup again.

Russell led the horse back to the group.

Calhoun sprang from his own horse. "Son of a bitch! Heathen savage Injuns got Kyle." He freed the body from the horse and let the corpse thud to the ground on its back. Jason Allen abruptly turned his head aside and vomited. The Mexican girl moaned and closed her eyes.

Russell dismounted and bent to study the fatal wound and the blood-soaked clothes.

"And you said Kyle would catch up soon," Smith commented.

Russell shook his head. "Not soon enough, I guess."

"God have mercy on his soul," Smith said softly.

Fury rose in Calhoun's eyes. "*You* ordered him to take up the rear, Captain."

"Adams got sloppy," Russell retorted. "He knew better than to wander off like that."

"Savage heathens," Smith muttered. "Lowest form of life is an Injun."

Allen looked anxiously at the horizon. "Captain, how many Indians do you reckon are out there?"

"Can't be a large parry," Russell said. "If it were, we would have been attacked by now."

"We've been in this country too long," said Smith.

"We're bound to encounter some settlements soon." Russell pointed east. "We're making progress."

"You call this progress?" Calhoun grumbled. "What about Kyle?"

"We bury him here, and then we move on."

McNally stepped forward. "Come on, J. D. Let's

give him a proper burial." The two men dragged the corpse away from the horses and began scooping out a shallow grave with their bare hands. Allen went to help as Smith pulled Russell to one side.

"What's our condition?" Smith whispered. "Be honest with me."

"I'm not sure."

"You'd better *try* to be sure. If we got a dead Ranger here and a party of Injuns on our back, the last thing we need is a doubtful captain."

"Well, something doesn't seem right," Russell said.

"What are you getting at?"

Russell shook his head. "That isn't the way of Comanches."

"Well, who the hell else would've killed Kyle? This is Comanche country. No one else lives out here."

"I'm not so sure about that. All I know is I've never heard of Comanches sending a dead body back like that." Russell paused. "Besides, did you see that wound?"

"I didn't get a good look."

"Too broad for an arrow and too thin for a knife."

"I'm not following your train of thought, Russell. You've been saying for days that these savages are following us. Now you're telling me it's someone else entirely. We can't take much more of this. These men are tired. They're half out of their minds with thirst and hunger, and J. D. is an especially wild card."

"J. D. and his kind are the reason we're out here to begin with."

"What do you mean by that?"

"Rich men like J. D's daddy just couldn't abide letting a horse thief run free," Russell said bitterly. "And a colored man at that."

"It's just the way of things."

"Well, it's a downright foolish waste of time and money." Russell glanced toward the horizon. Dusk was approaching rapidly. "We've covered hundreds of miles in and out of New Mexico territory, and for what? We never got our man. One of our own is dead. And we're stuck with that Mexican girl."

"You agreed to let them bring her along."

"Only way I could get them to keep their hands off her. I won't stand for rape in my outfit."

"That would make you a rarity among the Rangers."

"This is my unit. We'll do things my way." Russell sighed. "Besides, what can we do now? Just leave her out here alone to fend for herself?"

"It wouldn't be the first time."

"That might be other men's way, Preacher, but it ain't *my way.*"

Smith rolled his eyes. "Well, you're captain of this unit. *You* make the decisions. *I* only make suggestions."

Russell nodded. "That's reassuring, my friend. May I make a suggestion for *you?*"

"Certainly."

"I *suggest* you go say some prayers for our fallen comrade, and that we then get back on our horses and keep on moving."

Within a few weeks of joining Montoya's volunteers, Antonio had earned a reputation as a valuable scout. He knew the terrain around Santa Fe and could track a column of soldiers as easy as he could el cíbolo. It was no hard task to read in the break of a branch or the shape of a bundled chamisa which direction a quarry was heading.

As February gave way to March and then April, the federal armies waged a series of skirmishes and fierce battles against the invading Confederates from Texas. After seizing Albuquerque, the Confederates moved northward. Union forces had temporarily transferred the territorial capital to Las Vegas, abandoning Santa Fe to the invaders.

The tide turned at Glorieta Pass in the Sangre de Cristo Mountains. In what would become the decisive battle for the western territories, the Union forces managed to destroy the Confederate supplies, forcing the army of Texans to retreat south. The Union army had soon reoccupied both Santa Fe and Albuquerque.

By mid-April, Antonio was in Peralta, south of the Indian Pueblo of Isleta. He had tracked a column of Confederate cavalry southward, while Montoya's regiment approached the area from the north. Antonio soon learned that the Confederate army was resting among the cottonwoods and ranchitos surrounding the small farming village of Peralta. That agricultural community would be a welcome respite for the southern army after their retreat from the north.

Antonio and another scout were outfitted in civilian clothing and sent to study the Confederate position. Stationing themselves several hundred yards away, among tall green weeds watered by the recent spring rains, they eyed the hundreds of white tents. Groups of naked soldiers bathed in the nearby irrigation ditches. Antonio heard them laughing and muttering in the midafternoon sun.

"So they *are* here in Peralta," Antonio said.

"How many do you think?"

"At least four, maybe five hundred."

"And the rest of their army?"

"Probably headed toward the San Mateo Mountains, if Montoya's other scouts are correct."

"Montoya is already in Isleta," the other soldier said. "I can ride there in less than an hour."

"Good. Go now! I'll follow soon."

After his companion had departed, Antonio cast a quick glance around the horizon. Toward the east, the green Río Grande Valley gave way to a progression of brown rolling hills that would eventually merge into the snowcapped Manzano Mountains. To the south, Antonio could make out the outline of Tomé hill, a small mesa that rose above the villa of Tomé and the surrounding valley. Antonio remembered the Comanche raid at Tomé almost a hundred years earlier. He thought of his grandfather's cousin María Baca, who had been taken by the Comanche cacique. *So long ago,* he thought. *Such a different time and place.*

As Antonio turned toward where his horse was hidden, two shapes loomed against the bright sun. Two men in gray uniforms stood before him.

The taller soldier raised his pistol. "You best put your hands up in the air."

Antonio stood slowly, his arms over his head.

"Y'all understand English," the tall soldier said. "That's a good thing, boy."

"These people around here just speak mesican," the other soldier added. Antonio just shrugged in response.

"What are you doing around here?" the tall soldier asked.

"This is my home," Antonio said quickly, pointing to a small adobe house nestled among a row of cottonwoods. Several goats and cattle grazed in the nearby fields.

The tall soldier glanced at the house in disgust. "I don't know how you mescians can live in those mud huts."

Antonio said nothing.

The tall soldier said, "We're needing some help from y'all."

"I have my own fields to tend to," said Antonio.

"You best be getting your ass over there," the second soldier commanded, gesturing to the Confederate tents with his gun. "You've just volunteered to help us load up our supplies."

Antonio decided it would be unwise to argue.

The men herded him across an open field of dirt and

weeds, into the Confederate camp. They signaled for him to join a group of what were obviously forcibly recruited local laborers. Antonio saw hundreds of horses standing quietly in one part of the field. He also noticed several black people—slaves, no doubt—cooking and washing clothes.

For an hour and a half, Antonio helped load grain and other provisions onto ten wagons. He learned from the others that these supplies had been seized from Peralta and from the nearby villa de Los Lunas and the Isleta pueblo. Except for the tall soldier who stood guard, the Confederates paid little attention to Antonio and the other workers.

As the afternoon wore on, what had begun as a soft breeze grew to a windstorm. Gray clouds swept in from the Río Abajo and across the sun. The wind whipped dirt and dust into the men's eyes.

Then Antonio heard a crash and screams from a nearby adobe jacal. He looked up to see several raucous Confederate soldiers dragging two screaming, struggling young women outside. Antonio's fellow laborers glared in helpless anger.

The tall soldier laughed. "Just some of our boys having a little fun."

It was too much for Antonio to bear. He dropped his sack of grain and charged at the soldier. Caught off guard, the man stumbled backward, dropping his pistol.

Antonio yanked out a small knife hidden in his boot, plunging it into the soldier's stomach. The man's death cry was lost in the roar of the wind.

Antonio snatched up the soldier's pistol and aimed it at the Confederates by the jacal.

Then gunshots rang out from the north, followed by the thunder of hundreds of horses in full gallop. *Montoya,* Antonio thought.

The Confederate soldiers heard the noise too. Several hundred men poured from their tents and from the ditches. The ones by the jacal ran for their horses, forgetting the young women, who raced back inside.

The wind blew even harder; the swirling dust became blinding. Confederate cavalry assembled haphazardly as General Montoya's units charged in across the open fields, shouting, "Ándale!" Antonio squinted against the dust storm and saw Confederate tents and loose belongings flying.

As the wind died down slightly, he saw the Confederate soldiers galloping away to the south, Montoya's soldiers in hot pursuit.

For Antonio and the rest of New Mexico, the war would soon be over. Those of the Confederate cavalry who escaped Peralta rejoined the remaining forces in the San Mateo Mountains, but in several weeks, the invaders would leave New Mexico forever. Many months later, Antonio learned that the Confederates had marched into el Reyno with thirty-two hundred men, but that only fifteen hundred had returned alive. The dream of a "Greater Texas," and of a slave-holding Confederate States of America extending to the Pacific, was extinguished.

CHAPTER XXI

It was almost daybreak when Antonio maneuvered his horse down a sharp ridge about half a mile from the Tejano horsemen. Lucero, the morning star, glittered in the darkness.

The horse neighed as if asking for food and water. Antonio stopped and dismounted by a patch of small cacti.

You will be fed, my faithful friend. He took his knife and carefully cut away several small red nopales from the plants. Antonio stroked the horse gently while it ate the cactus fruit.

The moon still shone overhead, revealing the outlines of the Tejano camp. *Elena is with them,* Antonio thought.

Except for one man on watch, the party seemed to be asleep. Antonio sliced two more fruits from the cactus for his own breakfast. Its sweet juices were delicious on his tongue.

Everything a man needs to live can be found in the llano. No one with sense need starve in such plenty.

Antonio re-sheathed his knife, mounted, and nudged his horse forward toward the camp below.

Private Jason Allen shivered in the early morning air while his companions snored nearby. He perched on the flat surface of a small boulder that lay half buried in the earth, cradling his rifle in his lap.

Allen had struggled to remain awake during his watch. Despite the uneasiness that had haunted him since they had found Kyle's body the previous afternoon, he had drifted into brief dozes several times over the course of the night. If the captain knew about it, there would be hell to pay.

Allen scratched his beard and smacked his dry lips. The party was almost out of food and water, and he longed for a slice of beef or some freshly baked bread. Having that Mexican girl along hadn't helped; Captain Russell wouldn't let his men touch her, and yet he insisted on keeping her with them and sharing their meager rations with her. Allen cursed to himself. "Why in hell did I sign up for this duty?"

The truth of the matter was that he knew no other work. Allen's father, a farmer in southeast Texas, had relied on slaves to keep the farm afloat. With the end of the Civil War, the slaves were set free and the family lost its only affordable source of labor; they were forced to sell their land to make ends meet. Even then, the senior Allen had found feeding the family to be a constant burden. When Jason was only fourteen, his father had abdicated responsibility for him, walking the boy to a Texas state government building and volunteering his son for duty with the Rangers.

Allen shook his head in disgust and stared at the dwindling stars. He rubbed his forehead, desperate for just a few hours of sleep. Not likely that he'd get it. Once the others awoke, probably in about an hour, they'd have to pack their horses and move out quickly.

Allen glanced back at the camp. The Captain was asleep beside the dying campfire; the girl dozed nearby, her arms and legs still bound. The other men were snoring in their bedrolls. He considered waking the captain and pleading to be relieved, but decided against it. He stared into the darkness on the horizon, rapidly giving way to twilight.

Suddenly, a twig snapped nearby. Allen snatched up his rifle and held it at the ready. His eyes strained into the shadows. Nothing moved; there were no other sounds.

Just an animal, Allen told himself, but he gripped his rifle firmly. Cautiously he rose and moved forward into the darkness. He had advanced a few yards when another, crackling, noise came from a scraggly mesquite bush to his right. Allen spun around, aiming squarely at the bush.

A rabbit burst out and scampered away. Allen heaved a sigh of relief and turned back toward the camp.

Suddenly, he saw the shadow of a man creeping across the ground barely an arm's length away. "What the hell?" Allen shouted. He raised his rifle as the shadow spun toward him and a sharp pain shot through his body. He squeezed the trigger blindly as he collapsed to the ground. Seconds later he was swallowed by blackness.

The gunfire echoed in Antonio's ears as he ran for his horse, which he had left tied to a small tree a hundred yards beyond the camp. Shouts and cries rang out in the night as Antonio stumbled through the sagebrush and the llano grasses. He slashed through the rope and sprang onto his horse, galloping rapidly out of sight and gunshot range.

Antonio's heart pounded with fury as the horse flew across the dirt and rock. He had come so close! He had intended to slip into the camp and carry Elena away while the Tejanos slept. If only that sentry hadn't spotted him!

The rifle shot had not touched him, but he was feeling pain anyway—the pain of disappointment. Had he lost his last chance? He cursed himself.

By midmorning Jason Allen was buried in an unmarked grave somewhere in the llano Estacado. Russell and the remaining Rangers had moved on, but Allen's death hung over their heads. "They're picking us off like flies," McNally had growled upon waking to find the dead body.

The men guided their horses on over the lonely landscape. Calhoun and McNally shot frequent glares at Russell.

To ease his frustration, Antonio reviewed his memories of the days after the war. When he had returned to the Pecos Valley in early summer, he had found María and the children in good health, though they had eaten most of the grain and meat left over from the previous autumn's harvest. Now it was too late to do much planting, and María feared they might not have enough food to see them through the winter. There was no money to buy supplies, either; unlike the regular soldiers and even many of the gringo volunteers, few nuevomexicano volunteers had received financial compensation for their Civil War service.

Antonio planted what few crops he could, but he realized that if his family were to survive the coming winter, he would have to supplement their stores somehow. So in the early fall, he readied his horse for one last Cibolero hunt on the llano. María was concerned; she had heard much of the dangers Cibolero hunters faced, and she worried that he was getting too old for such work. To him, however, this chance to hunt again was not only a chance to put aside food for the winter, but the return of a lost love. Besides, he would be away for no more than a few weeks, just long enough to bring home sufficient carne seca for the winter.

Of course, things would be different in more ways than one. The great buffalo herds of Antonio's youth were rapidly disappearing, due chiefly to gringo hunters who killed for the sport of it. So long as only Indians and Ciboleros hunted the plains, taking what they needed to live on and maintaining a balance with nature to ensure that the cycle of life would continue as it always had, buffalo had been plentiful. But the gringos seemed to take pleasure in the ongoing, bloody decimation of the great herds. It was even said that the americanos' true motive was to subdue the Comanches by killing off their food supply.

Antonio could only shake his head in bewilderment and disgust at such stories. But at the moment, his most important concern was that the dwindling of the herds would make the cíbolos difficult to find, track, and hunt this year. There were still a few Ciboleros left, however, and they would be gathering at Bosque Redondo for the annual hunt.

Antonio rode his horse out onto the old familiar landscape of the llano. He traveled for several days, following the Río Pecos as it cut its way southeast from the La Cuesta region. By the time he reached Bosque Redondo and the Cibolero rendezvous site, his thirst for the hunt was at its peak. Perhaps some of his old friends would be there. *The years have passed,* he thought, *but not the memories.* A flock of geese flew overhead in an arrow-shaped pattern, as if pointing the way to the bosque.

Things were different even along the river. The immense cottonwood groves he remembered from his youth had been cut, leaving hundreds of stumps lining the sides of the river. Only a few álamos remained standing, their leaves turning gold and brown.

The afternoon sun was hidden beneath a sheet of gray clouds; a light chill hung in the air. Eager to rest before the anticipated hunt, Antonio galloped down a slope covered with dirt and wild grass, Now he could see the bosque from his horse. A number of men were already gathered near the banks of the river.

But . . . something was wrong.

Hundreds of men, women, and children were indeed camped along the river, but none of them seemed to be Mexicans. They were indios, a few Apaches, but mostly Navajos. What were so many Navajos doing here? Their domain was far to the north, west of the Sangre de Cristo Mountains. *They're very far from home.*

As Antonio rode into the bosque, he saw there were many more people here than he had originally thought. They covered the landscape as far as the eye could see. *There must be thousands here.* They stared at him blankly. Most were bone-thin; many of the children had bloated bellies. These people were obviously starving. Then Antonio noticed some of the Indians digging graves on the nearby hills. And he saw the men in blue military uniforms, surveying the encampment.

"Antonio!" a voice shouted.

Mañuel Luna, his old Cibolero friend, limped forward as Antonio dismounted. Mañuel, who owed his limp to an old Cibolero injury, stumbled up to Antonio and threw his arms about him in an abrazo. "It is good to see you, old friend."

"I had hoped I might find you here," Antonio replied. "But what has happened to the bosque?"

"Most of the trees were cut by the americanos to build a military outpost nearby. They call it Fort Sumner."

"And these people, the Navajos?"

"The army brought them here. The americanos have removed the Navajos from their homeland."

Antonio took another look at the americano soldiers. He recognized one man, who was clad in leather moccasins and beaver pelts. "Kit Carson," he said bitterly. Carson was much older now than when Antonio had known him in Taos; the trapper's beard had gone white and his skin was wrinkled. But the sight of Carson called up painful memories of Antonio's days in Taos.

"The Navajos have been here for months," said Mañuel. "Their leader, Mañuelito, and his band of followers are still holding out against the americanos in the northwest. Carson forced these men, women, and children to walk here."

Antonio raised an eyebrow in amazement. "They *walked* all the way here?"

"I only learned about it when I arrived in the area a few days ago. Our Cibolero camp has moved nearby, just over those hills. I saw you riding in, and followed you here."

"You there!" Antonio heard someone shout at him in English. He turned to see Kit Carson approaching. "Are you two with the army?" Carson asked.

Antonio shook his head. "No."

"Then what are you doing here?"

"Somos Ciboleros," Mañuel answered.

Carson scrutinized both men. "Buffalo hunters?"

"Yes," Antonio said.

Carson studied Antonio. "You look familiar."

Antonio just shrugged.

"These Indians are here to stay," Carson said.

233

"We're trying to make civilized farmers of them. We don't need you Mexicans getting in the way. Get out of here and go hunt your buffalo."

"But these people are hungry," said Antonio.

"They need to learn to fend for themselves, to plant their own crops here. We're gonna reform these savages into good Christians. You Mexicans should be glad; you're the ones who've been complaining for years about Navajo and Apache raids."

Antonio sighed and reached for his horse's reins. "All right, we'll be on our way."

Antonio and Mañuel made their way through the Navajo encampment. "Just over that hill," said Mañuel, "we'll find the others."

As the two men reached the outskirts of the Navajo encampment, someone said in Spanish, "Con su licencia." Antonio turned to see an old man with dark worn skin and jet black eyes, standing with his hand extended. A blanket woven in precise geometrical patterns was wrapped about the man's shoulders. "Can you help us? Do you have any food?"

Antonio pitied the old man. "I don't have much," he said.

"Anything, please."

Antonio reached into the brown leather bag hanging from his horse's saddle and removed the last of the hard tortillas de maíz María had packed several days earlier. He gave them to the old man. "This is all that I have left."

"Muchas gracias," the old man answered.

"De nada."

"My grandchildren will be grateful."

"I'm sorry for your troubles," said Antonio.

"We call this place *hweeldi,*" the man said. "It is a place of suffering. The white men forced us here on a long walk from our homeland in Canyon de Chelly. And we here are the lucky ones. Many of our old and feeble died along the way. The whites shot others who fell behind. Now they insist that we farm this desolate land, but our crops have died, and they give us nothing."

Antonio watched the old man walk slowly back toward the other Navajos. He followed Mañuel over the nearby hill to the small Cibolero camp.

At dawn the following day, the hunting party moved east from Bosque Redondo to the old cíbolo hunting grounds. Within two days, they found a small herd of buffalo grazing in the lands of the Comanches near el cañon de palo duro. Antonio and the other hunters managed to kill only a few buffalo, but Antonio did collect more than enough carne seca to see his family through the winter. After the meat was salted and dried, he took all he could spare to the starving Indians at Bosque Redondo before returning to his family at el cañoncito de Los Bacas.

CHAPTER XXII

Captain Russell filled his lungs with cool air as he laid the evening campfire. Above, the night sky was filled with calm gray clouds. A dark mass was forming in the east—the direction he intended traveling tomorrow. He sighed as he gathered twigs, grass, and other kindling.

"We'd all best be getting to sleep early," he told the others as they gathered about the campfire. He glanced at Elena, who sat on the ground nearby with a dejected expression on her face.

"I won't be getting any sleep tonight," Calhoun snapped.

"You ought to at least try," Smith advised.

"Not with those savages running around out there."

"Y'all will need all the rest you can get," Russell said. "Tomorrow we're riding long and hard."

McNally leaned over the campfire and stirred the contents of a small rusty pot. "This is the last of the beans," he said. "Captain, what's our position?"

"Maybe another day or two before we reach the settlements," Russell said.

"You've been saying that for the last week," Calhoun snapped, "and I haven't seen anything yet."

"Stop your bellyaching," Smith retorted. "We'll be home soon enough."

"No one goes on watch alone tonight," Russell said. "Is that understood?"

The other three nodded.

"We'll rotate in groups of two, and we'll all stay close to the fire. No wandering away from the camp."

"We're being hunted like animals." Calhoun's mind was still on the "savages."

"All the more reason to stay alert," Russell said. "Keep your eyes and ears open. We're almost out of this godforsaken wilderness. If we're going to make it home alive, we have to work together. Understood?"

Smith and McNally nodded. Calhoun made no response.

Russell raised his voice. "J. D., is that *understood?*"

"Yeah, Captain," Calhoun growled.

When Elena was six years old, Antonio had taken her on one of his seasonal trips to Las Vegas. It was the first time since they had left Santa Fe that Elena had been away from their small ranchito in the Pecos Valley. Like most of the area, the village of Nuestra Señora de los Dolores de Las Vegas had swollen with an influx of americano immigrants, though the majority of the population remained nuevomexicano.

As in most of the territory of New Mexico, the Anglos had built their own community, called "New Town," separate from the "Old Town" Spanish plazas of the nuevomexicanos. Antonio had visited a New Town general store on a previous visit to Las Vegas. The owner had been friendly and had asked Antonio to stop by again, so on this visit, Antonio came to the same store.

When they entered, he did not see the shop owner he

remembered. A gringa with a large face and short brown hair was standing behind the small counter. The other customers inside were all americanos.

"Can I help you?" the woman asked. Her voice was loud and shrill.

"I was here several months ago. The owner asked me to come back with more goods."

"My uncle? The old coot died of pneumonia last month."

"I am sorry to hear that," said Antonio. He paused. "Still, I would like to offer you some of my squash and corn."

"Wait a minute." The woman had seen Elena. "She can't come in here."

"Por qué?" Antonio asked.

The woman scowled. "Speak to me in English."

Elena shrank close to her father's side.

Antonio took a deep breath. "Is there a reason my daughter cannot come in here with me?"

"We only allow one Mexican in here at a time. New rules since my uncle died. Y'all need to take that girl outside, y'hear?"

Antonio shook his head sadly. "My daughter is only a child. And your uncle *requested* I visit again."

"My uncle was too kindly a soul for his own good."

"Never mind. I'll take my goods elsewhere." Antonio started to lead Elena to the door.

Then the woman glanced past him, out the front window at Antonio's wagon. "Wait. Is that your produce?"

"Yes."

Antonio saw the woman's face struggling between dislike of Mexicans and greed for his business. Then she sighed heavily. "Okay, you can trade here."

"Not unless my daughter stays with me."

The woman gritted her teeth. "Oh, all right."

Negotiations were difficult. The woman's dialect was different from the English Antonio had learned, and she did not understand the Spanish words he used when he had difficulty remembering English terms. But finally he left with several sacks of seed in exchange for his apples and vegetables. As he loaded his carreta to leave, he heard the woman say to another customer, "Someday the government's gotta require these people to speak proper English and outlaw that barbaric un-Christian language they speak."

Despite the unpleasant experience, Antonio returned to the store on several subsequent visits to Las Vegas. In time, the woman became friendlier and even began to learn some Spanish. Eventually, the store closed, and Antonio later learned that the woman had gotten married—to a nuevomexicano who spoke only Spanish. *Love can be strange,* he thought.

Still staring into his dying campfire, Antonio was jolted from his reminiscing by a faint noise from the large bush behind. He gripped his lance, rolled over with the weapon at the ready—and found himself staring down the blade into the face of a Comanche warrior holding a knife. The Indian stood motionless at the sight of the sharp and deadly point.

"Tell your friends to come out," Antonio said, doubting the Indian was alone.

The Indian hesitated, then nodded slightly. Three other Comanches appeared from the nearby bushes and weeds. Antonio saw their anxious faces clearly in the moonlight.

"You must kill me," the first Indian told Antonio.

"I have no intention of killing anyone."

"You hold the lance. My life is in your hands."

"You've traveled a long way looking for someone, but I'm not the one you seek."

The Indians were silent.

"You're looking for the men who killed your companion?" Antonio asked.

"You are the one."

"No." Antonio maintained a firm grasp on his lance. "I'm on the trail of the same men who murdered your companion. They carried off my daughter from our ranch. I've been following them for over a week."

The Comanches stared at him.

"I've killed two of their party. My daughter is with the remaining four. As soon as she is safe, we'll leave Comanchería." Antonio slowly lowered the lance. "I speak the truth to you."

One of the Indians walked to Antonio's horse and bent down to raise a hoof slightly. The horse neighed but did not struggle.

"This horse's shoes do not match the tracks of the murderers," the Comanche said.

Another added, "There was a woman among the Tejano party. This man must speak the truth."

"I only ask that you let me continue to hunt these Tejanos," Antonio said. "You may follow me if you wish."

One of the Comanches studied the lance in Antonio's hands and smiled, revealing a missing tooth. "This man carries the weapon of the Ciboleros. They are the best hunters among the white men. And we are long overdue at home." The others nodded.

"Cibolero, go and hunt your prey," said the Indian. "Our task is now in your hands."

Antonio watched as the warriors vanished into the darkness.

About a year after Antonio first took Elena to Las Vegas, a horse-drawn wagon rolled into the ranchito. Atop the buckboard rode a gaunt-faced man, a woman, and five children. They were obviously nuevomexicanos, and they all had desperate eyes.

Antonio looked up from where he stood repairing the adobe and wood walls of his torreón. The man stepped down from the wagon. "May we drink from your spring? My wife and children are thirsty."

"Por supuesto, señor. A su servicio," said Antonio. "You all may refresh yourselves here, and so may your horse." He called to María to bring food for the travelers.

The man introduced himself as Eulogio Gonzales.

"Where are you coming from?" Antonio asked.

"From San Jose."

"I know the village." Antonio had passed through San Jose a number of times on his trips to Las Vegas.

"We had to leave our small rancho," Gonzales explained. "Last week gringos came with some papers. They said the land was being homesteaded and we no longer had any rights to it. When we protested, we were forced off the land at gunpoint and with threats of death. They even burned our home."

Antonio remembered his own experience at Atrisco. "Yes, I have seen such things happen."

"Many of our people in San Jose are losing their land. Our people there are poor. The Americans are powerful, and the law is on their side."

"Where will you go now?"

"My wife has family to the south, at Bosquecito near Socorro. Perhaps I can find work in the americano mines near Magdalena."

As the men led Gonzales's horse to the nearby ojito for water, Antonio explained about his own lost land grant in Los Baca. "I have often wished I had fought back. It was good land. We were happy there."

"You did what you had to. No Mexican in this land has the power to fight the gringos."

"The injustice of it all never ceases to amaze me," Antonio mused. "These Americans preach democracy and equality, but they are concerned only for their own people. They have brought us nothing except misery and sorrow."

Gonzales nodded. "There is still talk of resistance in

Las Vegas and up in Mora. But I cannot join them. I have my wife and children to think of."

As Gonzales and his family drove away the next morning, Antonio told María of the conversation. "I wonder what awaits them at Socorro."

"I wonder if any land is truly safe from the gringos," María said. Her voice broke slightly. "I don't think I could ever face moving again."

A tear rolled down her cheek. Antonio put his arms around her and drew her close.

"Antonio. . . ." she said abruptly. "I am going to have another child."

Antonio smiled with happiness that masked a deep sense of uneasiness and anxiety. *What will the future bring to this family?*

In the weeks and months that followed, several other displaced nuevomexicano families passed through the canyon. Antonio learned that americano ranchers were raising fences of barbed wire across the vast land grants. Many families were forced to leave land they had farmed for generations, turning to work as shepherds or ranch laborers. Some of those who were allowed to stay on their farms became sharecroppers, required to turn over most of the land's produce to americano homesteaders.

Antonio began to think seriously about going northeast and joining the resistance.

CHAPTER XXIII

Russell leaned forward in his saddle and studied the torrent of water beneath the riverbank. The opposite side was lined with a thin grove of trees, beyond which lay rolling hills and a succession of towering buttes that merged into a distant canyon rim.

Maybe this is the Brazos, he thought. But it would be difficult to cross. Recent rains had swollen the narrow river, which was now plummeting with tremendous force toward the southeast.

Still, for the first time in weeks, he felt optimistic. *If this is the Brazos, then we're fast approaching home.* Surely the worst of their journey was behind them. Russell doubted the Comanches would risk venturing much farther from the Palo Duro. Since the days of the great Comanche raids had ended, the Indians were largely confined to the interior of the llano and farther north.

Russell signaled the other horsemen to dismount. He helped Elena down and untied her wrists so she could drink with the others.

All of them, including the horses, gulped greedily. Calhoun had thrown himself prostrate over the edge of the riverbank and dunked his entire head into the water.

"I never tasted anything so damned good," McNally said with a grin of satisfaction.

After their thirst was quenched, Smith stood up and

thoughtfully scanned the river. "You think this is the Brazos?"

Russell shrugged. "That's my guess."

"Then let's follow it," McNally said. "Ought to take us right home."

"It may not be that simple," Russell said. "There's still hundreds of miles of uncharted territory along the Brazos."

"Staying near this river sounds good to me," Calhoun said.

Russell thought a minute. "Even if we follow it, we're still days away from the settlements downstream." He checked the faded map from his leather pouch. "No help here. Assuming this is the Brazos, it must be the upper region. Most of that's still unexplored above Waco."

"And that country out there sure as hell don't look like Waco," said McNally. "Still looks like that shit hole we just came from."

Russell shook his head. "No, we have to be in Texas by now. But if that's the Brazos River, we still have a long way to go. We might encounter a settlement sooner if we go directly south."

"I say we stay by the river," Calhoun insisted and glanced at Smith.

"Maybe J. D. is right," said Smith.

Russell shook his head slowly. "No," he said. "I still think we're better off heading south."

"Let me see that map," Smith said.

Russell handed him the map. Smith scrutinized it

with a lowered head and squinted eyes. "Most of this region is still unknown. And we're not even positive that this river is the Brazos. Still . . ." He motioned the others around to see the map.

Russell drew in closer and placed his finger on the map. "Look at this. There are settlements down at the southern edge of the llano. We're probably far enough east that we could reach them by just heading south."

The men were momentarily silent as they studied the map.

Russell then said, "Besides, look at that." He turned away from the map and pointed toward the southeast, where the river seemed to merge into the remoteness of a distant canyon wall. "Looks like the river heads into some kind of narrow gorge. That'd be tough country to ride. We'll make better time by sticking to the high plains."

McNally nodded. "Makes sense. The sooner we get close to civilization, the happier I'll be. I don't reckon we can see any worse than we've already gone through, and I don't mind crossing more open country if it means we can see some white folks soon."

"What about them Injuns?" Calhoun asked skeptically.

Russell took the map from Smith and placed it back in the leather pouch. "If they're still on our trail, that's all the more reason to get out of uncharted country and close to the settlements as soon as we can."

Smith added, "God willing, we'll be all be home soon."

"All right," Calhoun said reluctantly and with a hint

of condescension. "We'll follow the good captain."

Antonio recounted how he peered through a moonlit night at a fence of barbed wire intended to prevent cattle from leaving the land—and intruders from entering. The sharp edges glinted under the full moon.

He watched his breath condense in the cold air. His mind drifted to Eulogio Gonzales, the refugee from San Jose he had encountered two years earlier. *I wonder what became of him and his family.* He was here partly in the hope of keeping his own family from ever facing a similar fate again.

He adjusted the white hood hiding his face and glanced at the thirty masked riders surrounding him. A pair of eyes—eyes revealing fire and desperation—burned through two holes in each mask.

The riders were a group of nuevomexicanos who had organized secretly to fight what was essentially a guerilla war against the recently arrived land grabbers from the east. Late the previous evening, they had gathered at a small ranchito near Tecolote—named for the many owls in the region—and from there had galloped through the darkness for hours to reach this place.

Now, the Sangre de Cristo Mountains to the west appeared as dark shadows in the black sky; unbounded plains sloped eastward into an opaque hue.

The horsemen dismounted and advanced on the fence. Two men began kicking at the wooden posts. Several others attacked the barbed wire with axes and knives. In minutes, the fencing was destroyed.

The riders quickly remounted and rode into the ranch, toward a large wooden barn at the top of a nearby hill. Antonio could see cattle grazing nearby. Reaching the barn, the men again dismounted.

They quickly gathered kindling and laid a small fire just outside the barn. Torches were lit and passed around. Then the horsemen threw their weight against the barn doors until they gave way.

Antonio, one of the first inside, noticed two horses in stalls. The horses whinnied nervously at the intrusion of the strangers.

Antonio opened the stalls and shouted "Ándale!" The horses bolted out of the barn and into the night.

The invaders quickly began setting small fires throughout the barn. Soon the whole structure was ablaze. The men ran to their horses and galloped away at full speed. Behind them, the burning barn glowed orange against the sky.

They rode for hours over open pastures, until they reached the forested hills surrounding Tecolote. There, they stopped to rest in a clearing surrounded by piñon trees. The crisp scent of piñon hung in the air.

The riders removed their hoods to reveal sooty, dirt-stained faces and eyes bloodshot with exhaustion.

The man by Antonio said, "We will meet up again tomorrow night. We have learned that there are new fences going up farther east."

Antonio shook his head. "I've been away too long. It's time to return to my family. I've done all that I can."

"But much work remains," the man said. "The ricos

continue to force our people off their land and close off the pastures of our land grants."

Antonio placed his hand on the man's shoulder and said, "I am sorry, my friend. But I must think of my wife and children."

"The americanos are powerful, but the word from here to Mora is that the ranchers are frightened by us."

"Then surely our raids have been effective?"

"Yes, we have done a great deal of damage to their interests, and we have accomplished much tonight. But although our allies in Las Vegas and up into Mora have promised still more support we continue to need all the help we can find."

"But I have been away from my family for two weeks."

"We can't convince you to stay and ride with us again, just one more night?"

Antonio thought a long moment, then shook his head. "No, I must go."

The other rider looked at him sadly. "Very well. We understand."

A few hours of rest later, Antonio bid his companions adios and turned his horse toward the southwest, heading for el cañoncito de los Bacas. He left behind a struggle that would continue on and off for years to come.

Fifty miles south of the river, the party of Rangers rode on over a landscape of mesquite bushes and cacti. As the day wore on, the ground sloped downward. The vegetation gradually gave way to vast fields of prairie grass, some of which stood as tall as the horses.

The grass swayed in the breeze like waves of water upon a lake. Russell watched several antelope dash across the distant prairie. *An unspoiled land,* he thought.

Smith drew his horse close to Russell's. "Any of this familiar to you?"

"Not yet. You have any ideas?"

"No; I've never been this deep into the llano country."

Russell shrugged. "We can't be that far from the settlements."

"I think we should take a breather right about now, wouldn't you say?" Russell looked at the exhausted, perspiration-streaked faces of the other riders.

"I suppose you're right. We've covered a lot of ground since leaving the river."

He signaled the party to stop. "Okay. Let's rest for an hour."

The riders dismounted. Calhoun began gulping from his canteen.

"Careful, J. D.," Smith warned. "Don't waste your water. Who knows how much farther we'll be riding today?"

Calhoun defiantly took another deep swallow before putting his canteen away. He leaned against his horse and leered at the girl. She turned away.

"Don't you turn your back to me, you damned greaser!" Calhoun exploded. He strode forward.

"Hold on there, J. D.," Russell ordered.

Calhoun ignored him, walked up to Elena, and slapped her across the face. She stumbled to the ground. "Por favor! No!"

"Don't go speaking that damned mesican around me!" Calhoun struck her again, this time with his fist. She collapsed, motionless.

"You'd best be getting away from her!" Russell demanded, drawing his pistol.

Calhoun spun toward his captain. Russell aimed his gun squarely at Calhoun's chest. "I told you to move away."

Calhoun glared back. "I'm through taking orders from you, Russell."

"You'll be looking at a hanging, J. D. We're only a day or two from the settlements, maybe not even that far," Russell warned. "There'll be a rope waiting for you."

"Somehow I doubt that will ever happen," said a voice from behind.

A shot echoed across the open plain. Russell felt a fiery blast in his chest as his knees buckled. He turned to see Smith standing with gun drawn, a thin wisp of smoke trailing from the barrel.

Russell collapsed numbly to the ground as his vision blurred. Blood gushed from near his shoulder; he could hear voices, but no words came through clearly. He forced his eyes open and struggled to raise his pistol at the shadows moving about him. His hand squeezed the trigger.

He saw one grainy figure drop before the world faded to black.

CHAPTER XXIV

Fresh horse droppings led south from the river. Antonio knew this region from his Cibolero days. The nuevomexicanos called the area el llanito verde and had hunted here for two centuries. The southward stretch merged into a great plateau upon which tens of thousands of cíbolos had once roamed. *But no more . . . the buffalo are gone.*

Antonio had followed the trail for half a day since leaving the river. Although heavy rains had recently fallen farther north, the region here was dry. But life continued on the llanito. A *bura,* a mule deer, scampered into the grass several yards away. To the right, several *tuzas,* prairie dogs, basked in the sunlight. The animals dashed into a shallow mound as Antonio passed.

Then the sound of a distant gunshot reached his ears. He pulled to a stop, listening carefully. There was a second shot, then nothing further—nothing but the soft rustle of the prairie grass in the breeze.

Antonio galloped toward the noise. The tracks he had been following led in the same direction. Ten minutes later, he saw dark objects on the horizon. He slowed his horse and approached cautiously.

The dark shapes resolved themselves into several saddled but riderless horses, milling about aimlessly. Antonio drew to a stop by the nearest animal. He looked down to see familiar horseshoe indentations pockmarking the area. Then, half-hidden in the nearby grass and weeds, he saw the body of a man.

Antonio dismounted to inspect the corpse. Then he heard the moan and realized another man was lying on the ground several yards away. Antonio walked over.

This man's shirt and overcoat were soaked in blood. He wasn't dead yet, but it was obvious nothing could be done. Antonio bent over him.

The man's words were barely discernible. "That damned Smith . . . some man of God."

"You're with the Tejano riders?" Antonio asked in English.

The man's eyes fluttered open and blinked in the sunlight, struggling to focus on Antonio's face. "Who are you?"

"My name is Antonio Baca."

"Wherever you come from, Mr. Baca, you must be a long way from home."

"This is my home," Antonio said forcefully. "And you have my daughter."

The man blinked again and his face took on an expression of anguish. "Your daughter? You . . . are the girl's father?"

"Yes.

"Not me. *They* have your daughter. . . ."

"Who are *they?*"

"The others. . . ." The man turned his head slowly and blinked at the other body. "McNally."

"That's the man who has my daughter?"

"No, not him. Not the dead man. The other two. The

preacher and J. D. . . . J. D. Calhoun." The man let out another shuddering breath and struggled to continue. "He was under my command."

"Who are you?"

"Travis Russell . . . Captain . . . Texas Rangers."

Antonio sensed that Russell was probably a decent man. Yet this was the leader of the group that had left such a trail of death and violence over the last week. "Why did this happen, Russell? Why did you let them hurt my family?"

"They were out of my control. They have no respect for anyone but themselves. They were about to rape and probably kill your daughter at the farm. I did the only thing I could think of to buy her some time." Russell's eyes slid shut, then slowly opened again. "Your daughter would have been released once we arrived at the settlements."

Antonio shook his head. "I doubt your people would have let her go."

"I would have tried . . . I swear. I would have done everything in my power."

Antonio glanced at McNally's body. "How many remain alive?"

"Just two." Russell spat out some blood and gasped violently. He clutched at his chest and whispered, "Your wife? And your boy?"

"They live."

"Good."

"And my daughter?"

"I think. . . ." Russell coughed violently. Blood gurgled from his mouth. "I think she's still alive. They rode off to the south. If you hurry, you might still catch them in time."

Russell's eyes closed again. "I'm so sorry . . . for what happened," he gasped. Then his body went limp.

Antonio laid the body on the ground. "I'm sorry, too," he said softly.

There was nothing more he could do here. Antonio stood and gazed at the southern horizon. The prairie extended for miles to a line of large hills and bluffs rising in the distance. Antonio swiftly mounted his horse and galloped alongside a series of clearly exposed horseshoe tracks.

"You done killed her," the preacher said, staring at the limp body draped over the horse. The girl's arms and head dangled loosely over the saddle. Smith guided his mount carefully with one hand, holding the reins of the girl's horse with the other.

"No," said Calhoun. "She was breathing when I put her on the horse. Maybe she's not hurt too bad." He grunted and maneuvered his own horse closer to Smith's. "A damned mess. Russell should have just stayed back and let us handle the Mexican girl."

"The Lord works in mysterious ways, J. D."

"And the captain?"

"He's not a problem anymore. I told you days ago he would have let her walk away the moment he got the chance. Personally, I don't think his other idea was too bad. If she recovers, we could still make a pretty penny selling her off to any brothel from here to Dallas. I've got a congregation to minister to back home, and some extra money will come in handy."

"What do we tell the Rangers about the captain and the others?"

"Injuns got 'em all."

"My pa won't be too happy. He was expecting to see a hanging in Waco."

"He'll have plenty to be happy about. He and the rest of those folks in Waco are still going to see you as some kind of a hero, surviving all that time in greaser and Injun land. And once we take care of the girl, you'll be going home with plenty of pay in your pocket."

"Still, I hate to miss out on a piece of that girl."

"Take her if you want. Just don't rough her up too much. We have to keep her presentable." Smith glanced ahead. "Well, what do you know? The captain had a pretty good sense of direction after all."

About five miles away, the plain gave way to several large buttes. The faint outlines of wooden buildings were visible beneath.

Calhoun grinned. "Well I'll be damned. The settlement's south of the river."

The girl moaned and stirred, raised her bruised face slightly, then slumped back down. Smith glanced at her as his horse suddenly slowed to a trot. "Whoa there, boy."

"Think he senses something out there?" Calhoun asked.

Smith shrugged. "He's just eager to get home."

"So am I," said Calhoun. "So am I."

Antonio spotted the two remaining Rangers only ten minutes after leaving Russell. Quickly he spurred his horse ahead and then around in a wide curve, until he reached a point about halfway between the oncoming riders and the Texas settlement ahead.

Antonio sprang from his horse and snatched the flint and chispa from the leather bag on his saddle. Crouching low, he yanked up a handful of tall dry grass and began striking the flint with the chispa. A small fire quickly caught and grew larger, sending up a thin plume of black smoke. Fed by the wind, sparks of orange and red danced furiously as the heat grew intense. Antonio's horse trembled and backed away.

"Easy there." Antonio snatched his Cibolero lance from the saddle. "Ándale!"

The horse galloped to a safe distance from the fire. Antonio stood alone, shielded by the height of the prairie grasses and the smoke from the rising inferno.

Fifty yards to the north, Smith sat on his horse with his mouth agape. "What on earth . . . ?"

The Rangers pulled their horses to a standstill. The prairie ahead was alive with dancing flames and soot. The wind blew the heavy smoke toward them, obscuring their view of the settlement ahead.

Calhoun squinted through the smoke. A rapid movement shot across his field of view.

"Did you see that?" he asked nervously.

"What?" Smith struggled to peer into the distance.

"There! Son of a bitch, someone is out there."

The men began choking in the surge of black smoke. Their horses neighed and danced wildly as Calhoun grabbed his pistol from his holster and aimed it in the direction of the fire.

The figure again moved into his field of vision. He fired wildly. The figure vanished, reappeared for a split second, then vanished again.

"I saw something!" Smith yelled, dropping the reins of the girl's horse. The animal began drifting to one side. "Over there!" Smith fired repeatedly into the approaching smoke.

"Did you get him?" Calhoun shouted.

"I don't know. I can't see!"

Calhoun suddenly realized the third horse had vanished. "What happened to the girl?"

"We've got a more immediate problem here!"

"I'm not losing her after all we've been through!" Calhoun galloped into the encircling wall of smoke.

Antonio had nearly reached the horsemen when the first broke away and raced toward where Elena's horse had vanished. Letting him go for the moment, Antonio lunged toward the remaining rider. With a snarl of rage and ferocity, the Cibolero burst from the smoke, his lance at the ready.

The rider screamed and leaned away as the horse bucked in wild panic. Antonio saw the man plunge from his mount to strike the unyielding surface of the llano headfirst. A crack sounded, the snap of a broken neck.

The man rolled over twice and lay lifeless.

Antonio rapidly surveyed the immediate area. He saw Elena's horse racing away in the distance. She was sitting upright now, but was having difficulty controlling the confused animal. The other rider burst from the smoke, rapidly gaining on her.

Antonio ran to the horse that had thrown the other rider. He leaped into the saddle, Cibolero lance in his right hand. The horse yielded to his firm grip, and he knew it was at his command. He leaned forward and drove his heels sharply into the animal's sides, racing toward the other riders at top speed.

Still dazed, Elena struggled to make her nervous, bucking horse run faster. She risked a glance over her shoulder and saw Calhoun approaching at top speed, fire in his eyes.

Suddenly, his horse stumbled. "Damn you!" he screamed, striking the animal violently as it struggled to regain its footing. Elena urged her horse onward, desperate to take advantage of the moment's delay.

Lance raised high, Antonio bore down on the Tejano. The man whirled, raised his gun, and fired. Quickly, Antonio rolled off his horse, still clutching the lance. He glanced up to see the man approaching, apparently distracted from Elena for the moment. Antonio lay motionless, waiting.

The rider stopped, dismounted, and pushed through the tall prairie grass. Antonio closed his eyes to a slit. The man stood over him and spat. "Damned greaser." He raised the pistol again, aiming at Antonio's head.

Antonio lunged upright, knocking the gun from the man's hand. He pressed the sharp point of metal against his attacker's throat. The man froze, his eyes widening with terror.

Antonio steadily inched the sharp metal tip along one side of the man's throat. He rose slowly to his feet, forcing the Ranger to his knees.

"Calhoun. . . ." Antonio said almost in a whisper, recalling the name the dying Ranger captain had mentioned.

"How . . . do you know my name?" the man stammered.

"That's not important. What is important to know is that you're about to die."

"Please . . . no."

"Do you know what this is?" Antonio asked calmly, nodding at his weapon. "This lance has killed many buffalo." He paused to lick his lips. "Have you ever seen how a buffalo is killed with a weapon like this?"

"Please, mister," Calhoun pleaded.

Antonio pressed the tip of the lance tighter against Calhoun's skin.

"I don't know you." Calhoun began to cry. "I just want to go home."

"My name is Baca. That girl you've been holding is my daughter."

Calhoun's jaw dropped. "How . . . where . . . where the hell are you from?"

Antonio gestured to the surrounding countryside with one hand, holding the lance on Calhoun with the other. "I'm from *here*. This is *my* homeland."

"I . . . I don't understand."

Antonio felt the weight of his past bear down upon him like the sudden onslaught of a flooding river. An impulse deep within urged him to plunge the weapon forward. He imagined the Cibolero lance thrusting deeply into Calhoun's body and blood bursting from the wound.

Buried visions from the past swirled in his mind: blood and death in Taos; the roar of the cannons; torn limbs and blood and dirt; his brother Felipe hanging from a noose; the battered body of his lovely young sister-in-law Petra; Mateo injured and unconscious; María's bruised face; the fear in the eyes of his little children; the sorrow in Joseph's voice. Antonio wanted revenge more than anything else. And yet, at the same time he was exhausted, burdened by years of hatred and resentment and regret.

Out of the corner of his eye, Antonio saw a lone horse approaching. Elena sat in the saddle. "Papa!" she shouted with tears in her eyes.

Antonio felt a surge of emotion overtake him. He wanted to cry and to shout for joy at the clouds and the sky. He felt as if a fever had suddenly broken.

"Please . . . let me live," Calhoun muttered, sobbing uncontrollably. "I want to live."

"Get up!" Antonio commanded.

Calhoun rose slowly to his feet.

"I'm tired," said Antonio, still holding the lance against the man's neck. Calhoun trembled silently.

"No more hatred! No more killing! Enough!" Antonio abruptly but carefully lowered the lance. "Go home and stay there."

Calhoun nodded numbly through his tears.

"If you or your people follow us," said Antonio. "I swear I'll kill every one of you. Do you understand me?"

"I . . . yes . . . I understand."

"Go back to your people and leave us in peace! Get the hell out of here."

Calhoun turned and staggered toward the distant settlement. As he disappeared from sight, Elena drew alongside her father. Antonio reached up to lift his daughter down from the horse. He quickly removed the ropes from her wrists.

"Papa," she whispered as they embraced, "I thought I would never see you again."

"We must go now," said Antonio as he saw his loyal horse standing nearby, waiting. "It is time to go home."

They looked westward toward el Reyno, to the beckoning call of the llano.

Epilogue

Antonio and Elena pushed through a narrow ravine of pebbles and sagebrush. The sound of surging water, combined with the smell of shifting mud and dirt, told Antonio that the river was near. The scent of fresh moving water penetrated his nostrils.

He leaned forward in his saddle and smiled at his daughter. "El Río Pecos," he said. "We're almost home."

Elena's shoulders sagged with exhaustion. "I wonder how Mateo, Benito, Anita, and Gabriela are doing."

"Your brothers and sisters are probably hurting, as is your mother," he said, then added reassuringly, "But they'll be fine. We'll be all right, Elena. You will survive these hardships. We all will, and our lives will go on."

They stopped their horses at the top of the ravine, drinking in the view of the meandering river and the valley below. "What about Pepé?" Elena asked.

Antonio did not answer immediately. He thought of the young Joseph Lewis and glanced again at his daughter.

"Please," Elena asked urgently, "what about Pepé?"

Antonio smiled. "Pepé is fine."

He feigned an annoyed silence, but felt his chest expanding with pride as he thought of the future. *Am I soon to have a pack of gavachito grandchildren running around my house pestering me? Perhaps I'll have to add more rooms to my house . . . or help Pepé enlarge his.*

263

Center Point Publishing

600 Brooks Road ● PO Box 1
Thorndike ME 04986-0001 USA

(207) 568-3717

US & Canada:
1 800 929-9108
www.centerpointlargeprint.com